# NSIDEOUS

ALPHONSO CLEMENT

Art By
ROB JR. IV

NEWMAN SPRINGS PUBLISHING
320 Broad Street
Red Bank, NJ 07701

First originally published by Newman Springs Publishing 2020

ISBN 978-1-64801-476-5 (Paperback)
ISBN 978-1-64801-477-2 (Digital)

Printed in the United States of America

To my past and my future.

# ACKNOWLEDGMENTS

I must thank my lovely and adoring grandmother, Ms. Eloise Watters, who loved me enough to courageously raise me as if I was her own son. She embraced me and uplifted me. She was dear to my heart and simply my rock through it all. I never got the chance just to say thank you.

To Patricia Chea, you changed my life completely and gave me a peace I never knew existed. I applaud you for remaining strong and maintaining a sense of loyalty. Thank you for not giving up and believing in me when others didn't.

To the two most remarkable women I have ever met, my wonderful sisters. I know growing up, I was a handful. No matter of our difference, y'all remained humble. Thanks for always having my back, either right or wrong. I'm extremely proud of y'all and love you with all my heart. I know it's been a bumpy road, with a lot of pain and misery along the way. I was back and forth from jail, in and out of prison, lost and suffering. But a struggle isn't forever, and a mistake doesn't define who we are.

Thank you.

# CHAPTER 1

The water was chilly, yet it was the month of May. Late into the night, the air slightly whistled upon the waves hustling against the shore. Suddenly, under the shadow of the moon, a man slowly emerged from the darkness of the ocean. He staggered a few steps before descending to his knees, imprinting his hands within the warmth of the sand. Blood was clearly visible on the man's soaked and pale skin, leaking from his head and slowly streaming down the middle of his forehead and across the bridge of his nose. The man was surely unaware of what happened. His body trembled, and soon he began to panic. He tried to speak, only to realize there was no vocal to his faint attempt. His mind was in a daze, filled with confusion, as life as he could recall just seemed to flash before him. Again, he tried to stand back to his feet, but he was completely numb. The little strength he did conserve would soon fade. He struggled to keep his eyes open, until they became so heavy he couldn't focus. With every blink was another tear, and every tear caused the world as he knew it to blur. His chest heaved, and then he exhaled softly unto total obscurity. His eyes were fixed upon a stare that was never to move again. It was as if one were looking into an endless light, a mirror reflecting only an image. For every death, there is a sense of something telling us everything we need to know. There's a moral to every story. You just have be the one to find it.

The next morning, a woman was walking her dog along the shore, when she came across the body of a man who appeared to have a gunshot wound to the back of his head. The thick dried blood had caked to his head, causing his hair to become matted. The bright pink color of brain fragments oozed outside of the quarter-sized hole he sustained at the center of his forehead. Her first instinct was to scream and run, but she noticed the dead man had something clutched in his hands. The woman cautiously scanned her surroundings and noticed nobody was in sight but her, her dog, and the lifeless man who laid at the tip of her red-painted toenails. This obscene scene wasn't unusual in her eyes.

Jessica McCray was born and raised on the grisly south side of Chicago. She relocated to Fort Walton Beach, Florida, two years ago after beating a federal drug indictment and a conspiracy to commit murder charge. Beauty was all Jessica had to show for her turmoil, not to mention the secret love affair she shared with her ex-boyfriend's cocaine supplier, Mr. Antonio Demarco.

Jessica knelt beside the man, carefully examining his facial features, and oddly as it may seem, death intrigued her. She always wondered what their last thoughts were. Did they suffer or was there any feeling of anything? Was it quick? Was there a sense of helplessness or sadness or even the thought of disappointment? It's often the understanding we get from things that hurt us the most. This is what had Jessica just stuck staring at the man and simply gazing into his eyes. There was something uncannily familiar about him, even though the hardened blood was sprawled across his expression. Quickly she dismissed the thought as being nothing other than a familiarity with death, or rather murder. She attempted to grab the cloth from his grasp, but it wouldn't give. The man's body jerked, causing Jessica to jolt back, startling her dog, who then barked hysterically.

"Shhhhhh." She considered her overly eager pet with a few gentle strokes on its head. Jessica nervously looked around again for any unwanted spectators before she commenced to prying his fingers apart until his grip released. Once what was held in his hand was now placed in hers. She regained her composure and eagerly unveiled its contents within her sweaty palm. What she discovered was totally mind-boggling.

Once she read the address written on the cloth, a skeleton key, a rare gold necklace embedded with precious gems, and a necklace that she knew belonged to her beloved mother. Her heart felt as if it fell to her stomach, her breathing was heavy, her hand began to quiver, fear overwhelmed her, tears burst from her eyes uncontrollably, yet a devilish grin creased the corner of her mouth. "Oh my god," she said only loud enough for her to hear. The streets were painted red from the biggest cartel war in American history, and here could be a piece of the puzzle that could possibly cease the bloodshed, or only make matters worse.

*****

Things weren't always so easy for Ms. Jessica McCray. Despite her stunning good looks and amazingly curvy body, there was more to her than meets the eye. But it took a certain type of guy to really see her for who she truly was. Jessica was used to getting her way, and nobody understood her better than Detective Kevin Winsten, homicide division.

*****

"Hello, baby," Jessica announced as she entered the million-dollar mansion she shared with Antonio Demarco. The mansion sat overlooking the very same beach where she discovered the dead man. Although the ocean view was a beautiful sight, no one would have ever thought a murder would occur at such a place. For every place that's considered a destiny holds something else, beyond what's naked to the eye is what you don't see, the truth under the lie in what we tell our self.

"Hello, gorgeous," Antonio replied. He walked up to her as his Gucci loafers inched across the marble tile. He eased behind her, wrapping his arms around her tiny waist. He embraced her tightly, and she smiled at his affection. His face between the small of her neck, he inhaled deeply. "You smell so good," he whispered before kissing her softly along her perfectly defined jawline.

Instantly, Jessica could feel his peaking arousal through his Gucci linens that were pressed firmly against her ass. She badly wanted to just bend over and grant Antonio the access he so desired, allowing him to smash her out beyond understanding. The thought of her matching his thrust while she threw her ass back had Jessica so wet she began to grind against him. Eagerly, she moaned a bit from the anticipation, and she became lost in the moment as she felt his bulge grow bigger and stronger. Yet she still couldn't completely get the thought of the man she found dead out of her mind, nor the thought of what the man held in his hand. *Who was that guy?* She pondered. *What was he doing here in Florida, right in front of our house? Why was he killed? Who was he connected to?* There were so many questions, but something wasn't right.

"Baby, oh my god, please, not right now," she pleaded. How bad she didn't want him to stop was clearly seen on her face as her eyes read of pure ecstasy. She unwillingly stepped away from him, but not before turning around to kiss him on his soft lips. She just couldn't resist to stare down at his lovely dick print.

"Why not? What's wrong?" He matched her smile. His eyes followed hers, and he attempted to grab for her.

"Nothing's wrong," Jessica responded playfully, as she quickly sidestepped his reach and rushed over to the other side of the love seat.

"Come here!" He gave chase just to feed the tease.

"Baby, no," she insisted.

"Okay, okay. Let's stop playing. What's wrong? Come over here and talk to me." Antonio sat down on the plush all-white Italian leather couch and poured each a glass of red wine. Jessica joined him, finding comfort as she rested her head on his chest. Antonio knew something certainly was bothering her, for he knew Jessica wasn't the type of woman to speak about her issues. She rather bottled things up and just acted like nothing what it seems to be.

"I don't know. Sometimes I'm just wondering if moving to Florida was the best thing for us." Her voice was at a faint whisper.

"Of course, it was. Why would you even question that? Look at all the heat you were under with the feds," Antonio replied as he lifted her chin, demanding her attention. They locked eyes, and he could see the strange tension reflected from her stare. "There's something you ain't saying. What's bothering you?"

"Antonio, there is nothing bothering me." She lied. Jessica sat up and took a sip of wine. She allowed her fingers to slowly trace through her silky hair, causing an awkward silence to occupy their space.

Antonio just stared at her from behind, observing while she nervously twirled a string of hair around her index finger, a distinctive sign he took notice of when Jessica was keeping something from him. "Baby, listen." She sighed. "Tonio, what's up with them Lopez brothers?" She shot a grimacing glance over her shoulder, which seemed to totally catch Antonio off guard.

He was completely bewildered. His eyes became like needles as he looked piercingly through Jessica with a stare that could penetrate her soul. His stare was very dark and chillingly cold. Jessica felt his energy and simply knew this was a subject she should have left alone. Often the things left in the past are left there for a reason. Unless you find your past catching up with you, then you must find some sort of resolution.

"Jessica, what about the Lopez brothers?" he asked. "Why are they even a concern?"

"I mean, Tonio, look at how we are living." Her head swiveled upon her shoulders. "We live in a f——ing million-dollar mansion. We constantly travel back and forth to Costa Rica just as much as normal people take trips to Walmart." She exhaled discouragingly. "Look at you." Antonio looked himself over curiously before exhibiting a manner of perplexity. "You own a platinum Rolex watch that cost a hundred grand, not to mention the hundred-thousand-dollar cars you drive up and down the Gulf Coast," she said emphatically.

"Okay, Jess, you say all that to say what?"

"You know what I'm saying," Jessica quickly replied before completely angling her body to face him.

"No, I actually don't." Antonio made no effort to hide his sarcasm.

"It's too much attention. That's what I'm saying. Too much unwanted f——ing attention, Antonio." Jessica's tone was full of stress.

Antonio extended his hand in an attempt to caress her face. Instead Jessica rejected his gesture by declining his reach. "I'm serious."

"Here we go again." He sighed agonizingly and tossed his arms in the air. "Come on, Jess. That's what all the investments are for, baby. Our books are solidified. Our lawyers and accountants work strenuously to keep the feds off our back. We good!"

"It's not the feds I'm worried about," she exclaimed. Antonio scratched his head in stupidity. "You don't seem to get what I'm saying." Antonio just stared at her. "Tonio, you are a major drug supplier." He swallowed his drink hastily. "Your best of friends are hip-hop moguls, athletes, and A-list actors. This is not smart, and certainly this is not how I was brought up in the game. It's too much, Antonio!" Jessica shouted before standing to her feet. Antonio attempted to grab her wrist, but she quickly jerked away. "No, don't touch me!" Her demand was daring.

"Jess, where is all this coming from? And what does any of that have to do with the Lopez brothers?" He arose from his seat towering, his six-foot muscular frame over Jessica while he awaited her response.

"It just feels like we are too comfortable, as if we are forgetting about what-ifs." She paused.

"What if what?" Antonio insisted.

Jessica's eyes diverted to the glossy marble tile upon where they stood. The smell of saltwater followed by a cool morning breeze sailed through the living room causing the sheer white window drapes to cast like a kite in the wind. Jessica's diamond-studded earrings sparkled from the morning rays. Her skin appeared so shiny and healthy with no hint of makeup; she was flawlessly beautiful. Antonio simply couldn't help but be captivated and a bit taken aback by the woman he has grown to adore. Jessica looked back at him with those dazzling eyes and completely found herself lost in lust with the handsome man before her. She struggled for words. Jessica just couldn't resist Antonio, his broad shoulders, his thick wavy hair, his strong, massive hands, and his enticing demeanor. Jessica embraced everything about him, even if it cost her in the end.

"Antonio, what if the Lopez brothers find us?" Jessica whispered desperately.

"I never realized we were hiding." He chuckled.

"And you find that amusing I see," she said before storming off, swinging her long luxurious hair and swaying her thick hips.

Antonio was tempted to add fuel to the fire but thought against it. He simply just smiled before retrieving his phone from his pocket. He was more concerned with what Jessica was talking about. The mere mention of the Lopez brothers had Antonio feeling edgy and a bit skeptical. Often, he really couldn't figure Jessica out. She had a keen sense with throwing people off-balance. Antonio was in urgent need of getting in contact with a man by the name of Julio Ceaser. Julio was a three-time loser from Delaware, New York, and also a captain within the Mexican drug cartel, a true man of honor and respect, yet ruthless at heart and with a militant at mind. He was a real cold, calculated killer.

"I think we got a situation," was the message beneath his fingertips.

# CHAPTER 2

Detective Kevin Winsten was nestled in a cheap motel on Miracle Strip Boulevard, high on cocaine. He picked through the bundles of cash spread on the bed. A Newport cigarette hung loosely from his mouth while it gradually smoldered. The smoke seethed a mixture of Cannabis streaming from the tightly rolled *cigarillo* that rested between Jessica's fingers. She sat peacefully in the shadows of the room. Her foot tapped at a racing rhythm. She was in search of understanding and drastically seeking answers.

"How much is this?" Detective Winsten inquired.

She replied dryly, "250,000." Then she added softly, "Thank you by the way."

"No problem." He winked. "But I was under the assumption after Chicago, we were done with burying these bodies." He looked at her peculiarly.

"And I was under the assumption that there was no questions asked. Nothing, right?" She steadily took a pull of the blunt, hindering the Jamaican funk in her chest. The smoke prickled at her lungs, almost bringing about a heap of coughs. She sustained against it, exhaling slowly.

"Those are my golden rules." He smiled. "It's a bit different when you are dealing with someone you have allowed yourself to cherish. There's more to it as being just business, but rather me caring," Detective Winsten explained. He inhaled the nicotine and exhaled the smoke through his nostrils. He ashed the rest of it in the ashtray beside the bed before snorting another line through a straw.

"I'm sorry, or rather, I apologize." She shook her head. "It's just this whole situation got me bugging. I don't know what to make of it, Kev. I really don't." Jessica's body was slumped in the chair, her arms resting across her breast, her face wearing a torn expression. She was utterly peeved.

"First and foremost, we need to find out who that guy was. I took a few DNA samples and lifted some fingerprints. Most likely this guy will be in the system. A name will tell us everything we need to know," he insisted.

"Yeah, make sense. That's good thinking. But for the time being, what else can I expect? Who else is there? That also means they know where we live. Even possibly watching our every move."

"All that's a possibility. But who is 'they' exactly? And, Jess, as far as your expectations, you can only expect what you allow yourself to expect. If you know something isn't right and something could possibly be a situation, you must think outside the box and simply reverse your chances," he philosophized.

"Oh my god. You're right, Kev. I wish Antonio was here. That was said perfectly. Damn! You really got me thinking." She focused on the jewels the detective just fed her mentally. Contemplating her next move, or rather her next conversation with Antonio, she weighed her options on so many different levels, even on the scale of the detective's behalf. Regardless of the secrets they may have shared and common grounds they may stand on, everyone has a price. Was Jessica rational? Not one person is exempt, not even Antonio. She cleared her throat, before reluctantly resuming in speech. "They, huh?" she exhaled intensely. "I'm referring to the Lopez brothers." Once she said that, Jessica surely aroused Detective Winsten's attention, his eyebrows arched in suspense. He and Jessica exchanged a taunting scowl, their eyes never shifting, nor blinking. There was a strong tension now filling the room.

"I don't understand." He hesitated. "I thought Antonio killed the Lopez brothers." Kevin Winsten's tone was full of uncertainty.

"That's what we thought too," she mumbled.

"Help me put this into perspective." He caressed his neatly trimmed goatee. "So who were the two bodies I buried that night if it wasn't the Lopez brothers?" he asked.

She winced. "This is where things get a little complicated."

"Complicated, how?"

"Well, actually, them two bodies just so happen to be the sons of a very powerful man." She paused to examine his bearings. "A murderous drug lord within the Medellin Cartel," Jessica solemnly continued.

"Say what?" he shouted. "No! No! No!" Detective Winsten was completely exasperated, his brows frowned between his eyes. He began to pace back and forth within the small space, chewing on his fingernails as perspiration began forming under his armpits. "Jessica, what the f—— did you get me involved with?" His wrath visible in his tone.

"Kev, please just calm down," Jessica declared.

"Calm?" he laughed sarcastically. "How am I supposed to be calm when you just said I buried the sons of a f——ing cartel drug lord?" he responded rigidly.

"Trust me, your name will never come up."

"It's not you I'm worried about. It's that f——ing Antonio I don't trust." Detective Winsten attempted to light another Newport, but his nervous hand vigorously caused the flame to flicker from his quivering lip. "What makes you think he won't hand us over to this cartel boss at the first offer just to save his own selfish ass?"

"In this situation, all you need is my word, Kev. Look at me," she demanded. He glared at her. "Trust me you will never be implicated in nothing." Her tone was sincere.

"Why am I just hearing of this?" He shook his head. "That's what's disturbing me."

"Honestly, I was hoping to clean all this up without bringing it to your attention. You know how embarrassing this situation is."

"Okay, so now what?" he questioned as the cocaine slowly drained down his throat and a cloud of smoke formed in front of his face. "What's on your mind?"

"Actually, I don't know," Jessica replied. "I'm thinking. I'm thinking." She diverted her stare toward the wall and simply just zoned out. She was trying to understand so many things, so many speculations, so many people she could point her finger at with not enough hands to do so. Wholeheartedly, Jessica knew she was in too deep the night she first had sex with Antonio. Then came the plot against her ex-boyfriend, which eventually led to his murder. Now Antonio being negligent in his expectations has pushed Jessica into an unsettling predicament. His lack of concern has driven her to mental exhaustion, ultimately infuriating her.

Detective Winsten looked out the partially closed curtains as he lingered in thought to the memory of his childhood, a picture painted so vividly. It was a small reminder of the ties his mother once shared with the cartel, when she used to smuggle tons of cocaine and millions in cash across the Mexican border. Before he was detective, he was just Lil' Kev. Lil' Kev grew up like the rest of the lower-class citizens, simply poor and trying to make a way. He walked down the harsh reality of New York City in the direction of his mom's domicile, a place in his mind he never looked forward to going, where the deplorable memory of misery reluctantly remained. After his uncle's murder, things just weren't the same. Lil' Kev was more so holding onto a piece of his past that he was willing to forgive but never forget.

His Timberland footwear graced the asphalt. He noticed the transition in his borough, the addiction that crack and heroin influenced. It was an alteration he really couldn't attempt to feel any type of compassion, for he definitely wasn't resolving the problem, but rather adding to the circumstances rebelliously. Slowly analyzing the panorama, he saw helpless souls staggering past empty baggles and crack vials that cluttered the pavement, abandoned buildings, and blood-stained streets where dreams shattered. The life of futility, the land of evil, this bock he roamed was indeed in the devil's palm.

Entering his mom's apartment, a sense of uneasiness came about him, crinkling up his spine and causing goose bumps to emerge as he noticed the extinguishments and sedated movement, a picture so unfamiliar behind the doors of these quarters. His mom would customarily be accompanied by her crack-induced accomplices, scrambling up funds over scraps like a cluster of rats. He was used to seeing the consistent empty stares of faces encrusted with dirt, shame, and disgust. Often that foul aroma of crack being charred reeked through the air. Obviously, something was off.

Without any more hesitation, Lil' Kev retrieved his cherished .380 caliber from his waistline. Slowly he made his way to the kitchen with his pistol honorably aimed firmly in front of him, but nothing seemed to have appeared besides the usual roaches that scattered soon as he flicked on the light switch. Making his way back to the living room, there was nothing out of the ordinary; it was the same messy suite five days ago. He stood looking perpetually down the hallway, forcing his eyes to adjust the writhing sensation that had his heart palpitating abnormally. Attaining his advance up the hall, a pungent stench overwhelmingly hit him. Lil' Kev couldn't help but gag while his eyes started to scorch impelling a trickle of tears to roll down his cheek. His stomach begun to coil as he felt that McDonald's Big Mac and six-piece nugget preparing a violent eruption. With his free hand, he took the collar of his shirt and covered his nose with the possibility of preventing the abominable smell. "What the f—— is that?" he managed to utter. Mindfully, he placed his back to the wall, serenely sidestepping down the hall.

At the age of fifteen, he really didn't know what to expect. Usually the foul smell of decaying rodents would always fill the air from alleyways and overflowing dumpsters. This was deemed to be different. Lil' Kev reached the doorsill of his room, and surprisingly the door was still secured. Normally, it would be wide open due to the indecency of his mother and her snooping-ass friends. Releasing his shirt, he peered to the right of him to survey the other end of the hall as far as he could perceive. Slowly turning the circular knob, he pushed open the door in a swift motion with the assistance of his pistol sturdily extended. From corner to corner, he swept his arm. Understandably his nerves seemed to be getting the best of him. The heat and temperature mixed with the sensibility of the unforeseen caused his nose to sweat. Undisguisingly getting caught slipping was his worse phobia, though as an adolescent Lil' Kev knew karma had something in store for him.

Nothing seemingly of concern as he gained entry of his room, immediately he diverged into the bathroom. From there, he backed up the hall to his mom's room. Oddly her door was slightly open, which automatically refreshed his memory of that stringent night he witnessed his uncle murdered. That awful smell grew stronger as he stood stiff in front of the bedroom with his gun now down at his side, feeling as though he couldn't go any farther. His legs appeared to be so light to the point as if they weren't even attached to his body. Something eccentric within him like a voice of some sort was telling him when that door opens, he should expect the inevitable. He exhaled heavily before bringing forth what was sustained behind curiosity. What stalled him mentally, his eyes couldn't perceive clearly, and his expectation was that this was all just a figment of his imagination. His heart felt like it submerged into his abdomen after seeing his mother stretched out naked on the bed, her throat slit from ear to ear, her tongue dangling from her neck, blood covering all four walls of the small room, even from the ceiling to the floor. The words to express what he was experiencing while his mom's confused flesh blanketed a thin film over his vision was 0 to none.

Killing sometimes could be committed without any thought, but when death is on the other end and close to one as one's bare skin, it's much harder to endure. Seeing the horrific scene painted a mental picture so vivid he just remained motionless, embedding an instant rage of suicidal tendencies racing through his brain. He grasped the handle of his .380 in the sweaty palm of his right hand, slowly tracing the small lever with his index finger, daring to initiate an action off impulse to fade his existence to an unknown darkness. Lil' Kev couldn't even shed a melancholy tear from his scrutiny. His knees becoming incredibly weak. His hands commenced to unnerve, fluttering uncontrollably causing his gun to descend from his grasp to the floor with a blustering thud. Lil' Kev was replete with agony. Emotionally he became filled with a sense of guilt nobody on God's green earth could understand, a pain that seeped so deep he couldn't gather himself. His heart was torn. He was just stuck in his stance. The betrayal of his mother's innocent blood weighed heavily on his mind. The devil appeared disguised in its many faces, developing in many shapes, crawling through the veins, and intruding the minds of innocent souls to unleash its evil from the plant of a seed. And within that shell, attentively Lil' Kev stood.

*****

"Um, hello? Is anybody home?" Jessica shouted. "What the f——, Kev?"

"My fault, Jess. I just had a lot on my mind," Detective Winsten replied before turning back around.

"You and me both, you think?" She rolled her eyes. "But, aye, I need you to focus. I can't afford for you not to have your head in the game," Jessica said.

"Nah, I'm all right. I'm here. What's up? Where were we?" He smiled sheepishly.

Jessica just looked at him for a moment. She could tell he was experiencing one of his many episodes but decided not to speak on it. "We were discussing the murder of Antonio," Jessica stated coldly. "Well, actually, that's what I was talking about, seeing that you weren't paying attention."

"As you were saying," he insisted.

"I got too many wrinkles I need to iron out, and what better way to start than with the one who got me in this f——ed up situation?"

They exchanged glances, and then silence ensued. "How? What's your plan? I mean, c'mon now, this is Antonio Demarco we speaking about."

"Huh?" she chuckled. "Why do you say it like that?"

Detective Winsten looked more confused. "Say what like what?" His palms were displayed upright at waist level.

"You mentioned his name as if he was John Gotti or something." She squinted. "Never mind that. My plan is giving Julio the contract on Antonio," she said encouragingly.

Winsten nodded his head in agreement. "Julio Ceaser I assume."

"Yes. You know of him?" she questioned.

"No, not exactly. Just heard of him." He looked away from her momentarily before looking back in her direction. "Are you sure you can trust this Julio guy?"

"Honestly"—she held the side of her head in her hand, her elbow resting on her thigh—"Kev, I don't know who I can trust. I don't have no other option though."

"I'm saying, Jess, logically do you think the dead guy on the beach had some sort of connection to Antonio?" He eyed her suspiciously.

"I really can't say. Right now, I don't know what to think." Her gaze lingered toward the floor.

"So why kill him before finding out what's really going on? A dead man is useless if it's answers you are looking for." He took the credit card off the tabletop and commenced to fix another line from the pile of cake.

"I'm not taking any more chances with that clown. If it is, it is, and if it ain't, it ain't. If it's ever a toss-up between me and him, it's going to be him before me," she stated firmly before advancing to her feet and flinging her long hair toward her back. "You sure do seem to have a change of heart. Not too long ago, you didn't trust him. Now you're trying to spare the guy." Jessica shook her head in disbelief. "This is so f——ing incredible!" She paced.

Winsten smirked. "It's not that I'm sparing him for the reason that I give a f——. More so because there is a lot that's not making any sense to me at this moment. Something is telling me he is better off alive than dead. That's what I'm saying." He leaned forward and inhaled the white substance off the wooden surface and quickly held his head to the ceiling as he snorted and sniffed, allowing the drug to settle.

"I'm not about to sit around twirling my thumbs as if this sh—— is amusing. I'm removing everyone who I consider to be problematic, the same resolution my father would have recommended," Jessica declared earnestly.

"Yeah, but your father isn't here to recommend anything. I am! And I am because I gave him my word that I would be. Now, I'm not in a position to tell you what to do. But I'm going to tell you like this. If you kill Antonio, that means you have to expose yourself as being the head of this organization. Is that something you can handle?"

Detective Winsted caused Jessica to halt in her tracks. She appeared to have taken what he said into consideration. Nevertheless, she responded, "I've been handling it. You think these m——s don't know? I'm the fabric and stitching to this outfit." Jessica vigorously slapped her hand against her chest. "I ain't got to hide behind anybody. These m———s are going to respect me just as they respected my father." She urged, "Trust me, Kev, Antonio won't be missed." She looked him up and down, shifting her weight on one side of her hip, displaying that whole Chicago attitude. "Are you in or out?"

"I see you're real adamant about this situation. If that's what you think will be your best move, then move with precision. Apparently won't nothing I say change your perception." He obtained the duffel bag and stuffed the stacks of money back inside. Then he seized his .45 Luger from under the pillow and adjusted the pistol concealing it in his lower spine. "Your father often walked through life only hearing what he wanted to hear, rather than hearing what he needed to hear," was his statement before exiting the room.

Jessica truly couldn't understand why Detective Winsten was so agitated. Suddenly, the ringing of her phone broke her stare from the obstruction at the door. Rushing over to the nightstand, she picked up her phone and glanced at the screen. It read, "Julio." She sustained a peculiar look.

# CHAPTER 3

Jessica and Antonio were lying on the couch watching *New Jack City* on Netflix and engaging in small talk about business and life. Antonio held Jessica close to his bare chest while he massaged her scalp. Something suddenly eased into his thoughts that caused his manhood to alternate in his boxers. Jessica felt his firmness as it pressed into her stomach. She just modestly smiled and pleasantly looked up at him.

"What is it you're thinking about?" Jessica bashfully inquired.

"You and this big ole thang right here." Antonio smacked her on the ass and grinned charmingly.

Jessica accepted his naughty gesture and diligently pulled his erection from its snug enclosure, taking possession of it with a tender touch. Steadily and meticulously, she stroked his dick, playing with it, caressing it between her hands. A light moan eased from her mouth as she enjoyed the peak of his ponderous pulsation. Jessica sprang into action by slowly licking up his shaft like it was a melted ice cream. She allowed her ferocious tongue to tickle the tip of his dick, which caused Antonio to groan and move about in this position. She had him captivated, and she unquestionably knew her head game was impeccable. The glee appeared in her eyes as she peered up at him, and then she spit on his throbbing flesh before throwing her lips to it and commenced to sucking desirably, coinciding with her hand moving relentlessly in a circular motion on his extremity. Abruptly she stopped and pulled his dick out of her mouth and fervently slapped it on her tongue. The lust of it all was amazing and totally transparent in her tantalizing effect that sounded from the back of her throat. Jessica took back to it, slurping and sucking with persistence while she fondled with his genitals. She was making love to his dick, showering it with an abundance of affection. She enjoyed it. The whole aspect of it being in her mouth turned her on conclusively. Antonio was getting harder and harder, his genitals becoming tighter, and he squirmed excitedly. Jessica knew he was about to ejaculate, as bad as she wanted him to cum in her mouth, just the taste of the warm sensation. And the weakness in his body was so stimulating to the thought. Out of nowhere, both of their phones began to ring and vibrate simultaneously with three solemn knocks at the front door.

"What the f——? Who is it?" Antonio yelled, quickly fixing his improper exposure before he rushed from the couch. Completely oblivious to the loaded Glock .45 directly in reach. He mumbled a few more obscenities as he snatched open the door, again allowing his rashness to ignore the bushmaster AR-15 that was posted up beside the door right at his side. He neither once looked through the peephole nor even bothered to ask who it was. He didn't take notice of the oddness in their phones ringing at the same time nor the fact that it was late into the evening. Soon as the door passed the threshold Antonio was settled in a fixed stare, a silencer was placed sternly to his forehead from a small-caliber weapon. Instantly brain matter burst from the back of his head, and he dropped right where he stood. The only sound that came next was that of a coin dancing on the floor from a hot shell casing dislodged from the chamber. The masked gunman made entry. Firmly in his stance, he lowered his weapon suspending it over Antonio's heaving chest. After a brief moment of indecisiveness, he released three more projectiles that muffled the air like a needle to a balloon, perforating his torso as blood seeped from his wounds. Satisfied the gunman looked up spotting Jessica standing there irresistible in a red thong and a red baby doll tee revealing a glimpse of her perfectly critiqued body. Her expression was blank, meaningless, as the man's eyes seem to have protruded from his ski mask lustfully. Unbeknownst of the spark of interest Jessica reached over the Glock .45 and retrieved an already open pack of Newport. She shifted one out, placed it between her voluptuous lips, and lit it. She inhaled deeply and then exhaled slowly. She compelled his attention courteously and he just nodded his head slightly embarrassed. Jessica reciprocated the nod nonchalantly, after which she simply vanished. Advancing on his departure was another mystic figure dressed in all black displaying a roll of plastic under his arm, a variety of cleaning agents in one hand, and his other contained a handsaw, was no other than Detective Winsten. She smiled broadly as he shut the door softly behind him. Jessica spun on her heels posing angelically staring out the window of her ocean view while she puffed heavily on the nicotine that engulfed her lungs.

"Please don't despise me." She sighed gravely.

"Why would I?" He sat his things down and casually unrolled a lengthy piece of plastic right alongside Antonio's corpse. "Surely not because of this guy." He pointed toward the floor where the body laid. Then he became temporarily speechless as he stated greedily at Jessica's marvelous heart-shaped rear. Instantly his hormones caused an unexpected urge to grow enormously in his Michael Kors jeans. The utterance of Jessica's voice intercepted his thoughts.

"I don't know. That's what it sounded like back at the motel." She kept her eyes trained on the water below her, dwelling on so many situations that she seemed to be facing by the second. "What are the odds?" she pondered. Shaking her head, she remained focused, back to the subject at hand, as she strategically diverged her thoughts.

"Of course," he chuckled. "But it wasn't meant to be taken out of context." He awaited her response. Silence persuaded another sentence. "You were my concern. My interest was to at least question the guy." He slipped on his latex gloves. Jessica ignored his comment blatantly. Detective Winsten sighed vexatiously. *This woman can be so stubborn*, he thought to himself. He commenced to roll Antonio's body upon the plastic where he meticulously disrobed him of his jewels and personal fabrics. Clasping the sharp-toothed instrument firmly, he placed it to this throat, grasping the top of Antonio's head with his other hand, like the palm to a basketball. Soon as the teeth was about to rip through Antonio's flesh, Jessica's syllables eased from her mouth.

"When playing chess, would you ever consider a stalemate just as triumphant as a win?" she asked furtively.

Detective Winsten stood upright bewildered, the handsaw swinging loosely at his side, overstepping Antonio's body. Slowly he paced himself down the hall of exquisite art and paintings, bypassing the huge tank containing two massive hammerhead sharks, and then angled himself parallel to Jessica. Her stare never shifted.

"That's an interesting concept." He nodded his head impressively. "It all depends. Sometimes life may present obstacles that mean more than a victory." The detective placed the saw at his feet and detached the latex gloves from his hands. "Jess," he called out before forcibly rotating swiftly her petite frame. "Lessons are useless if you never use what you were taught. You speak of a stalemate, but a win is nothing if it's an ungrateful win. To stand victorious is all in the heart."

Jessica politely and authoritatively suggested he remove his hands from a mere shift of her eyes. The detective obliged without hesitation. Jessica looked up at him fiercely before redirecting her mental concentration back outside. The detective was flabbergasted. Jessica overlapped her arms across her stomach and then exhibited a peeved expression. Detective Winsten dispiritedly gathered his discarded gloves and saw from the floor as he began to walk away.

"Hey, Kev!" Her words caught his back. Naturally he stopped as he peered over his shoulder. Jessica observed his reflection through the window. Realizing she had his attention, she resumed, "Do you tend to always take from the dead?"

His face unthinkingly twisted into an expression of displeasure. He stared at her briefly and then took heed of the diamond embedded jewelry that was stuffed in his pocket. He produced a cunning smile and said, "Ain't nothing wrong with a little memorabilia." The detective chuckled as he progressed in his stride. "Besides, what is he going to do with it?" He glanced down at Antonio's lifeless body. "Look at his brains! I would say jewelry is something he wouldn't be complaining about." He enabled a sinister laugh.

Jessica's mind was spiraling out of control, but rather than contesting her thoughts with Detective Winsten, she fetched her silk pajama pants from the floor. After shimmying the soft fabric over her curry physique, she spoke. "Never mind him. I want you to dispose of his body in the anaconda pit," Jessica demanded. "After which, tomorrow about twelve noon, I want everyone to be where they need to be. I got a few things everybody would want to hear."

The sternness in her eyes let the detective know she meant business. "Whoever isn't in attendance as I expect them to be, the consequence of their defiance is death."

Detective Winsten agreeably nodded as he tightly rolled Antonio's bloody corpse in the plastic. He peeked from his position where his eyes locked into Jessica's looming glare. Sensing the hostility, he attempted to console her temperament. "Jess, you all right?" he questioned suspiciously.

She looked at the detective strangely and simply replied with a nod of her head.

"It just feels like there's something you refuse to say," he suggested further.

"Kev, maybe so. Maybe what I got to say isn't meant for you to know. As you said, everything isn't for everybody."

"Yeah, but…" The detective spun back around after retrieving a thick roll of duct tape to secure the plastic covering Antonio's body. That's when he noticed Jessica was no longer there. Suddenly, the shower sounded in the distance followed by the soft tunes of the song "T-Shirt" by Destiny's Child.

# CHAPTER 4

Jessica quickly silenced the heavy chatter as soon as she stood to address the room. "Listen up, fellas!" She patiently analyzed the perspective of each individual. "Antonio is away on assignment."

Unconsciously she locked eyes with Julio, which automatically caused him to become uneasy. Immediately his eyes diverged to the right of him with a frowned expression.

"But it's still business as usual," she continued. "We can't ignore the fact that there is a war between cartels and the Lopez brothers are still a major problem with our distribution. We are losing shipments about 26.2 million. That's not even including our Dallas and Jamaican contacts." Jessica spoke to the clustered room of six hustlers, four professional killers, two captains, and three lieutenants. Everyone was attentive and very much anxious, embracing every word dependently.

*****

Jessica was arguably the most ruthless gangster on the female aspect of the game. She was known equally for her good business sense and for her sociopathic tendencies. Jessica was the daughter of Fernando, a kingpin hailing from the Dominican Republic. Her mother was Jamaican with a mixture of West Indian blood, which explains Jessica's nationality and exotic features.

At the peak of her parent's livelihood, they were unspeakably murdered in a double homicide outside an ice cream parlor in the middle of Manhattan when she was just fifteen. The circulation of conversations said it was behind a failed extortion plot by the Russian mob. Others assumed differently. Another conversation said that Fernando became so large in the borough of Queens, New York, he created a heap of envy. His stubborn and cocksure demeanor caught the attention of the Mafia, not to mention the criticism of the streets. There were so many speculations that she eventually stopped entertaining the absurd assumptions.

Jessica moved in with her grandparents after her mother decided one night to leave Chicago to be with Fernando—or rather chase this fancy and flashy sense of a guy when Jessica was a blooming thirteen-year-old. As a young girl, she was confused while she adopted to her new circumstances without the daily interactions of her mother and father. Nevertheless, her parents played a major role in her life even from a distance.

Jessica was what you would consider as spoiled. She had the best of everything. Anything she wanted, she got it. Fernando's perspective was to shower her with gifts to keep her mind off the things that usually derive around explanations. Jessica was a witty girl. She heard a lot and saw much more than expected for a young woman. Everything that was intended to discourage her away from the life of the hustlers only seemed to intrigue her, though she couldn't comprehend the art of hustling beyond hustling the small quantities of cocaine she pitched at school, after finding a quarter brick tucked off in the basement of her grandparents' house, along with fifty thousand in cash. Basically, Jessica was more concerned with fitting in with the other rebellious kids and most importantly catching the eye of a boy who sold crack on the corner down the street from her bus stop. This boy was her ex-boyfriend Fabian, who she would eventually manipulate to sell her drugs.

At the spike of Jessica's drug-dealing odyssey, Detective Kevin Winsten made himself familiar, after a brief run-in with Jessica when she was busted with two ounces of cocaine inside her gym bag at the house of a triple homicide. Detective Winsten was best friends with Fernando. Before he joined the force, he was Fernando's personal bodyguard, not to mention hitman. He always told Fernando if anything were to ever happen to him, he would watch over Jessica unconditionally. So naturally when he discovered what was stashed in the bag, he knew what was expected of him and simply introduced

Jessica to the Mexican drug supplier. At the age of twenty-one, she embraced her inheritance, a multimillion-dollar drug empire.

*****

"So, Jess, what's the plan? Because that's a big lost. That's two hundred bricks of product we going to be stuck with," a disappointed voice announced from the inconsiderate crowd.

"The plot is simply to regain our revenue and at the same time focus on killing these f—— Lopez bastards." She scanned the cold stares, spotting a sign of skepticism within the eye of one of her lieutenants. "We can't allow any of what's going on to hinder our progress. Around 80 percent of the cocaine sold in America is coming from our contacts in Mexico. So is 14 percent of the heroin and majority of the weed. Just in case any of y'all seem to have forgotten how imperative our positions are here," Jessica declared as she looked from left to right, in search of uncertainty or a sense of guilt, ultimately wondering who had the nerve to comprise her entitlement. The deed was daring. Her father would say, "People aren't always who they appear to be." Jessica was taking that into consideration, along with the realization of the possibility that the feds could be lurking.

It was always a thought of things coming into question due to her father's legacy. Outlandishly, as if being a woman presiding over a corporation of manic killers and a million-dollar a month flip with a mathematical crew of hustlers was virtually impossible, Jessica's true perfection of life was her exceptional good looks. Again, her beauty belonged on a canvas, defined by the finest paints and oils and to be traced with the softest bristles, a gentle touch, and a flawless arch displayed by the wrist. Extraordinary is far a better description. Her innocent features were most intriguing, but what's noticed from the outside often covers the innermost being, the things and thoughts that derive from ideas and circumstances, that dark place in one's soul that people tend to conceal through smiles and simple laughter. To look a person in the eye means more than just a look. It's a peek inside of a world colder than winter. One would see things that are not often seen, faces unfamiliar, the pain and hurt reflected from a scorn expression. It's called the truth, or reality, and this is what Jessica is striving against as the energy in the room became slightly tensed.

"But, yo! All that's cool. That's mad respect. But I'm confused. How did them Lopez brothers even catch on to how we was moving to even start intercepting our product in the first place?" Julio managed to say through a sly grin while he slouched in his seat chewing on a toothpick.

"Actually, I don't know." She shrugged her shoulders. "It's obvious someone told them, and that someone could be anybody. Rather than trying to figure that out, we got to keep the money moving. An explanation is unacceptable when it comes to over a million dollars' worth of product coming up missing." She paced back and forth to the window, stealing glimpses outside. "Changing up our routine is mandatory and keeping everything limited to who knows what," Jessica assuredly declared.

Julio just nodded, grinning devilishly.

"Bet!" The man rubbed his palms together. "That sounds like a plan, darling, but wise. They say some of the best lessons are the ones taught in blood." The guy sitting next to Julio said.

Another man cleared his throat. "To my knowledge, I was under the assumption that this whole issue of dramatics was honored by Antonio Demarco personally," the older gentleman said. One could tell he was a bit flustered from the profound look in between his bushy brows.

Jessica giggled. "Yes, it was something that was intended to be carried out by Antonio. As I said, he's away on other business. So I'm not in any position to speak on his behalf." She stared unflinchingly at the man. "What I can speak on is this." Jessica transferred that striking glare over to Julio. "Julio, you are now in charge of the shipments. This means you will oversee who does what, who's driving what car, who makes the switch, where, and when. You will be in control of the product from when it reaches us all the way down to the dealers on the corner." Julio nodded his head agreeably with a wink of the eye.

Jessica ignored the absurd expressions in the room and narrowed her attention to one of the young killers standing modestly against the wall. "You and your guys will be responsible of tracking down these Lopez f——s and killing them wherever they stand. This is what we are going to do." She momentarily gathered her thoughts. "We are going to set up a dummy stash, keep everything the same as it already is, the same mule, the same location, and the same route. Not only will it feed off their greed if they were to bite on it, but also if they don't at least attempt it, flushing out the traitor should be easy."

She scanned the room and lifted her perfectly trimmed eyebrows. "To everyone else, we going to drop the prices of our product and simply reduce the cut." The room immediately erupted into heavy chatter. "Yes, of course we will lose a bit of profit, but the idea is to monopolize the situation. It's nothing we can't get back. My main factor is to keep the supplier of this operation satisfied," Jessica stated clearly and directly.

Of course some things didn't sit right with a few, but they understood it wasn't worth speaking on. Everyone in attendance gained their composure and acknowledged one another's departure as they headed toward the door. Julio lingered around waiting for the room to clear. Jessica noticed his demeanor being real edgy, eager for her attention, so she made eye contact with her body guard as he observed near the doorway. Jessica nodded her head to excuse his presence.

"So what can I help you with, Julio?" Jessica's expression coincided with her tone of voice. She was stern and to the point.

"I just wanted to make sure everything was good between us," Julio whispered while slowly advancing toward Jessica.

"Why wouldn't it be? I don't understand." She seemed confused as she took a step back from his approach.

He shrugged his shoulders. "I don't know. Just curious." Julio continued his progress toward her.

Suddenly, Jessica's back hit the wall, a gasping moan escaping her lips. Julio's hands commenced to roam patiently and steadily on her shapely thighs to the outline of her thick hips. Jessica's body tensed under the touch of his fingertips. His warm breath graced her lips while they stared intensely at each other.

"You mean to tell me that night never crossed your mind?" he teased before slithering his tongue out like a snake, enticingly licking her bottom lip and creating a tingling sensation to sustain between her legs.

"Julio!" she sternly placed her hands on his chest, hindering his persuasive intentions. "This isn't a good idea," Jessica strongly insisted.

"It was then. What's the difference?" he spoke confidently.

Jessica had to admit she admired his persistence, not to mention his aggressiveness or the fact that he was a handsome guy who so happened to have f——ed her in ways a woman never considered possible. Quickly she brushed past him, fighting the temptation of wanting this man to bend her over and be f——ed as Julio so desired.

"The difference"—Jessica softly explained, as Julio spun around, mischief displayed on his appearance—"is a drunken night, a mistake in judgment, enraged hormones. Your dick just happened to be at the right place at the right time. Nothing more."

"Are you sure about that?" Julio urged.

She laughed hysterically. "Say what?" Jessica looked at Julio in a haze of mystique. "So you were under the assumption with you killing Antonio was a hint of me wanting you?" She shook her head disappointedly. "That explains your reason of recording that conversation on your phone. You knew I was going to kill Antonio after hearing that." She sighed. "And here you are thinking off some simple sense of sexual desire that only seem to exist in your own foolish mind." Jessica became furious as she just stared at Julio through squinting eyes. *The nerve of this guy*, she thought to herself.

Julio's embarrassment prevented his speech. He stood there as if he was unconscious.

"Julio, I think it's best if you excuse yourself from my presence." Jessica walked over to the door and snatched it open, awaiting for him to leave accordingly. Her eyes veered toward the floor, since she couldn't even stand to look at him any longer.

Before his foot crossed over from carpet to concrete, Jessica had one last point to make clear. "Business means everything. Pleasure is nothing more but a moment."

# CHAPTER 5

One week later, Jessica and Detective Winsten were enjoying each other's company on a remarkable afternoon aboard her late father's $2.5 million yacht, navigating through the Gulf Coast. Jessica anticipated the need to unwind, considering the suspicious activity of peculiar-looking vehicles sitting idle in front of her residence, the strange phone calls in the middle of the night, and the people she had never seen before jogging the neighborhood and walking their pets along the beach. Jessica was surely a nervous wreck. A peace of mind was essential to her train of thought. Besides, it was her father's day of birth. So this was a typical celebration between her and Detective Winsten that they brought forth every year. They paid homage to the man they both seemed to have loved and admired dearly. On a more personal level, Jessica also suffered from manic depression. She just felt the need to get away. Mentally, she wanted the boat to continue forward endlessly. Nonetheless it was all just a figment of the imagination.

Meanwhile the detective maintained a chilled demeanor, appearing handsomely striking for his age, and Jessica couldn't help but adore his persona while secretly gawking at his neatly groomed salt-and-pepper hair, his strong and mature facial features, and his overwhelmingly eye-catching structure. Being a devoted daddy's girl, she had a strong attraction toward older men. A cunning grin appeared at the corner of her mouth while exclusively analyzing the many characteristics of the detective she earnestly seemed to seek in other guys. Sadly, no one has ever compared to the man before her, nor to the man her father was. She just stared into his discouraging and slightly alarming eyes. They were empty and clearly seen as mysterious, which he was. He was an unpredictable sort of a man, just as Fernando was. Jessica sensed he had a lot weighing on his mind due to his state of tranquility and mere standoffishness, as he stared bleakly off in Jessica's direction.

"Are you seriously going to be mute the entire time? Kev, you're making this awkward. Just spit it out. What's up?" Jessica announced through a twisted expression.

"Wouldn't you at least think there was enough going on without you devising a plot to murder Antonio? His position was more valuable than I think you care to know." He shook his head. "Jess, questions are being asked, and I have to be the one who answers them." The detective's back rested against a twenty-four-carat gold railing. His defining arms folded across his strong chest, his legs smoothly overlapping the other. His stance was cool, laid back, and demanding.

"So that's what this is all about?" She laughed softly. "I thought we already cleared the air on that situation."

"It's different circumstances when the prospect is bigger than me and you. When you mentioned Antonio Demarco, people seemed to stop and listen. You were sadly mistaken when you assumed he wouldn't be missed," replied the detective.

"Okay, wow! He turned out to be someone of importance." She applauded obnoxiously. "Way to go Antonio Demarco. Who would have ever imagined?" She rolled her eyes with disgust. "Everybody wants to be somebody, though it seems you ain't nobody until somebody kill you," she responded.

Detective Winsten gave her an absurd look. "What's that supposed to mean?" he stated before cutting his eyes away from Jessica and the casually lighting the hand-rolled tobacco stick that was concealed fashionably in a gold cigarette case.

"You rather spoil my father's remembrance with some frivolous sh—— like this instead of just praising the moment. What's done is done," she lashed out. "Speaking of which, remove these f—— things off my father's boat and out of my sight!" She hinted slyly with a gentle push toward the black trash bag, assisted by the tip of her red bottom heels.

The detective glanced down at the bag and then swiftly cast his eyes across the open waters. He tugged the heavy bag to the side of the yacht. Detective Winsten emptied the contents of severed heads into the deep blue ocean below. He braced the edge of the boat, watching as the four faces of Antonio's personal henchmen get whisked away, including the head of a gorgeous Armenian woman who was rumored to be Antonio's mistress. The most disturbing fact that ironically caused the detective's gaze to linger was the notion of the woman was six months pregnant. Jessica wasn't taking any chances. She knew she had to take action. Detective Winsten understood Jessica had the capability to annihilate an entire nation if she chose to. He flicked the partially smoked cigarette midair as he diverted his stance.

"Look, Jess!" He moved back toward her. Trying his hardest to conceal the annoyance written on his face, he said, "It's not about spoiling anything. It's all about gaining a sense of knowledge in why things happen the way they do. That's what this is about."

"You tend to make everything sound so easy, as if things are just that simple." She giggled. "Come on, Kev, you of all people. If you were in my shoes, you would have responded in the same manner," Jessica said.

"But you are reacting off an assumption rather than purpose," the detective replied.

"I had every purpose in the world, and you don't even realize it," she insisted.

"What I do realize is having Antonio killed before making him talk was such an idiotic decision if you want to be truthful."

Jessica looked at him querulously. She was astounded that he would say such a thing. The detective appeared oblivious toward Jessica's perplexity and simply resumed his discussion. "Jess, you just defeated the feds at something people usually don't overcome. You do know they have the highest conviction rate, right?" Jessica agreeably nodded her head. "You did all that without being a f——ing rat. For you to gamble against the odds and put yourself out there all over again, Antonio was the perfect façade for this operation and ultimately keep you in the shadows. I just don't get it." The detective's voice was trembling. "As much as I hate to say it, if you keep thinking naively and not being able to decipher who's with you rather than against you, Jess, you're going to find yourself in a situation you can't handle."

Jessica couldn't seem to form any words to express what she had on her mind. She quickly yet casually disguised the damage in her eyes behind some designer frames. She angled her body away from the detective to face the bustling water, the wind catching her hair like a flying kite. The briskness of the breeze tingled her face, and it was as if Jessica was in a trance. She relaxed her breathing, engulfed by the peace and the slight calls of the ocean as its waves splashed rhythmically against the sailing yacht. The calm caused Jessica's thoughts to become dreamy, just as Julio seemed to have intervened with a soft glimpse of a mere fantasy.

*****

"Well, Fabian should be home in a second. I'm about to take a shower real quick. I'm sorry I'm a little tipsy." She laughed. "You need anything, a drink or something, while you await?" Jessica questioned allowing her soft almond-shaped eyes to lead Julio astray from his normal thinking.

Knowing this wasn't a line he wanted to cross, especially with Jessica secretly messing around with Antonio Demarco, he just shook his head as the weed smoke slowly exhaled through his nostrils. Julio strained his attention on an old mafia flick displayed on the movie projector ahead of him. Yet he couldn't reframe from eyeing Jessica's curvaceous backside bulging out from her jeans. She walked off vanishing toward the rear of the house. Julio sat patiently anticipating the arrival of Fabian just to put a bullet in his brain, under the strict orders of Antonio Demarco of course.

Within a few minutes, Jessica returned to the den completely naked and dripping wet. "Excuse me." She giggled. "This is so embarrassing. I'll just be a second," she said slightly bent over rummaging through a duffel bag.

Julio was stunned. His eyes almost popped out of his head amorously. The fire burned desirably in his mind. He wanted her, always have. His determination fed his ego. Julio needed her. Confidently he stood from his seat and boldly walked up behind her, grabbing a nice feel of her ass where he thought his fingertips were going to disappear into her soft skin.

Jessica jumped, spinning around swiftly where the finely trimmed hairs of her pussy ultimately enticed and intrigued Julio. Despite Jessica's confused expression, Julio progressed. He began to touch her intimately, allowing his hands to roam adventurously. Jessica didn't make any attempt to stop him nor showed any sign of resistance. Looking into her stare, it was all so evident, so immediately he dropped to his knees. Julio knew he had to grant her full control. Jessica was a different breed, and he had to approach things in a unique manner. Jessica ran her hand through his thick curly hair. Just as she lifted her leg, propping her foot on a small table stand, Julio softly kissed her pussy lips. Before he began to gently suck on them, she moaned ecstatically as she tugged at his hair. Using two of his fingers, he spread the meaty pair of flesh between her shapely thighs, popping out the pretty pink, hardened clitoris. Eagerly Julio placed his tongue there and began guiding it up and down in a slow motion while greatly savoring her taste.

Jessica grabbed the top of his head securely to catch her balance, as Julio had her trembling in her stance. The power of the tongue indeed was a force to be reckoned with, as Jessica's legs became weaker and wobblier. She was so enthused from his creativity. He commenced to sucking and kissing on her swollen bean. The delightful sounds instantly escaped from the depth of her throat. Julio proudly devoted his mouth to her graciously, enjoying every bit of what she had to offer, from her raspberry smell to her luscious taste. He inserted his index and middle finger ever so gradually inside her thoroughly soaked passage of endearment, moving them in a circular motion at the same time as Julio tickled her underlying sensation with the tip of his flickering tongue. Jessica's grip tightened with a fistful of Julio's hair, and her exhilaration grew stronger just before her legs began to twitch, which Julio knew she was about to climax, encouraging further his sexual execution. Eagerly wishing, he felt the warm sensation of her juices flowing like a slow ooze all over his mouth and face. Suddenly, she crumbled to the floor, curled up into a ball, with her hands in between her thighs while she shivered from the tingling sensation like a cold breeze. Abruptly, Fabian entered the dimness of the room chattering on his cellphone. Julio jolted to his feet as Jessica scurried amidst the shadows, humiliation quickly settling. Yet an explanation wasn't feasible, and a spent round soared through the air, striking Fabian in the head.

*****

Jessica quickly retracted from the disturbing images, as her pussy throbbed annoyingly. She uncrossed her left leg from over her right knee just to formally cross her right leg over the top of her left knee, as she composed her demeanor. She looked toward the detective who was staring off into the remoteness while indulging a plate of sushi.

"Kev, I can't say you ain't right, and I didn't mean to inconvenient things. Maybe I was thinking a bit selfish, but the structure of this organization is my top priority. I'm a boss, and being a boss, executive decisions are made, oftentimes hurting people in the process, whether mentally or physically. It happens, and it happens because it's supposed to. Come on, Kev, ain't no heart in this business. You told me that," she spoke appealingly as she poured herself a glass of wine.

"Well, in response, I think you should know. Not that I'm disregarding anything you're saying, but your dead guy." A reluctant pause occurred while he chewed his food.

Impatiently Jessica compelled his halted speech. "Okay, and?"

"His name was Devecchio."

"Devecchio," she repeated.

"Does it ring any bells?" the detective questioned. Jessica pondered. "Allow me to answer that. Devecchio was one of the mafia's most feared killers." Jessica agreeably nodded.

"He was associated with the Colombo family back in the day. I don't have any issues with any of the five family organizations. What was his reason in being there?"

She stared back out toward the water, as she thought back to her mother's necklace and address that was clutched in his hand. She shook her head spitefully. "This sh—— is getting more confusing. What the f—— is an old-school mafia hitman doing roaming the backyard of Fort Walton Beach?"

"I can't say. The thing is if this Devecchio was such a prolific figure, who killed him?" the detective replied.

"F—— who killed Devecchio!" Jessica uttered in a loud tone. "If he wasn't killed, then what? That's the answer I'm looking for." Jessica dismissed the glass she was occasionally sipping from and suddenly snatched the bottle of chardonnay and tossed it back consuming a big gulp. A deep minerality and a pleasant earthy finish rested in the confines of her throat.

"Jess, if we can put a name to his killer, everything else might just make sense. It might just shed some light on this whole situation, because a man of his status doesn't just get murdered and no one knows about it," he said calmly between bites of sushi. "Of course, only if it's something you think I should know, as in if it's something you are not telling me," he quickly insisted, trailing off his last sentence with a devious grin.

A peculiar feeling cringed at her spine, for she knew Detective Winsten was hinting at something, a revelation she didn't have any intentions on baring. Jessica was very much aware of his sharp sense in reading people and his ability to find the truth in a lie just through mere conversation. The man was a homicide detective to say the least, not to mention his keen sense of the game. He been around in his forty-five years and met people only some could imagine. From eating lobster and shrimp with top bosses of the most elite crime families to his reputable association with cartel and mob figures, Detective Kevin Winsten was among the legendary hustlers, kidnappers, and killers. His corruption was initially about surviving, making money, and getting ahead. As time passed, he got addicted to the money and power, just as most of people do.

"No." She laughed deceivingly. "There is nothing I need to tell you. You just think you know me, huh?" She exhibited a broad smile.

He shrugged his shoulders and raising his eyebrows. She mimicked his ludic behavior and said, "What's that supposed to mean?"

"It simply means I don't need to know you." He snickered. "But I know you enough, just enough to know who I'm dealing with. Does that make sense?" His tone was stern.

Indeed this was her father figure, the man she looked up to and highly respected. So she listened and took heed to his every word. Nevertheless, there was just something hindering her from telling him the truth. As bad as she wanted to, her hips just couldn't form the words properly. Jessica knew his intentions were good, and that was the logic she reminded herself subconsciously. There was a reason Devecchio was there, and Jessica firmly believed it wasn't to commit an act of violence, yet to warn her of something or someone. Coincidentally, that same someone or something silenced him before he got that chance. It was just a suspicious indication, as Jessica hunched toward the detective.

"Yes, it does," she replied in a childish manner. "Can I ask you something, Kev?" she asked in humbled tone.

"Of course, you can." He appeared shuffled. "What's on your mind?"

"Every time I refer to the incident concerning my father and what led to his murder, oddly you won't ever tell me what actually happened. You seem to always speak around the subject. Why is that?" Jessica sat there analyzing his adoring features, wrenched in a sneering expression.

"Jess, I tell you only what you need to know and what I know to tell you. Honestly, I don't know what the situation was all about that led up to anything. You got to trust me on that. I have no reason not to tell you if I did know something," he stated.

"I guess," Jessica murmured.

"Excuse me?"

"Nothing!"

"Okay, since we're in such a generous mood to ask questions, let me ask you something." He quickly tossed back a shot of Johnnie Walker. Jessica slowly removed her glasses and sardonically glimpsed at the detective. "Why don't you ever speak of your mother as you do your father? It's as if her murder doesn't even exist. You can't despise her that much."

"Don't do that!" she said sternly. "There is no need to ever mention anything about my mother again." Her stare was piercing. "Me and my mother are a whole different story. You know the bond was I shared with my father. Kevin, I can't believe you just said that." Tears overwhelmed her as she jolted to her feet and vanished below deck. The detective smile cunningly.

"I'm always a step ahead of you," he whispered.

# CHAPTER 6

Spanish Harlem was the home of Daz Juan Costello, a mild-tempered, laid-back sort of guy. He was real reserved and very much not talkative, but when he was in conversation, literally there was something worth saying. Daz Juan was in control of the drug scene throughout the Spanish Harlem, even to the palms of hustlers up in the Bronx.

In July 24, Jessica and her entourage of exotic-looking ladies flew out to Atlanta to enjoy a birthday bash of one of her friends at the famously known establishment. Entering the dimly lit atmosphere, they appeared to have stepped into a pictorial for a smooth magazine. Hair, makeup, and attitude all marks of high intelligence, ability, and achievement. Everything about these women spoke volumes. They demanded attention, from their Gucci pumps, Louis Vuitton bags, and diamond-studded jewels. These women were groomed by gangsters and hustlers, the type of dames accustomed to shopping overseas, Europe, and Paris, spending $5,000 on a bottle of wine, pushing the pedal of a Maserati and Ferrari SUVs. This flock of beauty was the true definition of boss bitches.

Upon entry, the place was utterly amazing. It was everything it was rumored to be and even more than she imagined. At first glance, Jessica took notice of all the big-booty, tattooed women twerking on stage. One was popping in a handstand, while another pair were on their hands and knees making their ass cheeks clap together simultaneously. A bunch of guys showering large denominations of cash on the women formed into a voracious crowd. The raunchy lyrics of Young Dolph blasted throughout the club. Jessica couldn't really define just how deliciously attractive these young and vibrant strippers were. It was all so overwhelming. The artfulness, the variety, and the immense number of asses were amazingly enough to make any woman lose control. Jessica's eyes widened with curiosity and showed a shimmer of excitement. The group of ladies proudly eased through the packed and smoky room, glowing provocatively from pink and blue light bulbs. The scented smell of pussy trailed in the air as overly passionate females teased and flirted, flaunting their perky breast and lustfully lifting their legs straight in the air, causing their meaty thighs to jiggle vigorously. Beer and liquor flowed freely, along with platters of hot wings on paper plates and palms full of molly. Suddenly, the music stopped, and without delay, all the dancers collected the massive amount of sprawled-out bills before clearing the stage.

"Hey, how y'all doing out there?" The crowd yelled and applauded rambunctiously. "This is the place to be. History in the making. The hottest joint in the A right here. Big ups to my man Costello of this fine establishment." He waved his hands in the air, hyping the crowd even more. "Hey, let me give a bigger ups to the lucky birthday girl Armani." The boastfulness was clearly seen on Armani's face. She glanced over at Jessica smiling sheepishly.

"I know you out there somewhere," the DJ teased as he placed his hand above the brow of his eyes scanning the cluster of people. Another friend of theirs earnestly snatched Armani's wrist and raised her arm high in the air while they giggled. "There she is." He pointed.

Armani politely waved to all the spectators looking in her direction. "We got a special treat for you!" he shouted energetically before spinning off Cardi B's number one single *Bodak Yellow*. Armani gleefully started to gyrate her thick hips toward Jessica, brandishing a zealous expression. Just as Armani embraced her childhood friend and whispered words of appreciation in her ear, the DJ swiftly blended into another one of Cardi B's hot tracks, just as the vocals of the rapper aggressively ripped through the microphone. The whole club jumped into a small frenzy once Cardi appeared, causing everyone to rush to the stage, including Armani as she slightly pushed away from Jessica, unable to conceal her friendly obsession of the young beautiful Bronx native. The stage was once again overwhelmed with dancers, bouncing their ass boastfully. Cardi couldn't contain herself from all the hysteria and gladly appeased her fans by arching her back, palming her knees, and twerking her bulky derriere indefinitely.

Jessica stood in the distance, vibing to the beat, as her body seemed to have tingled in a sensational manner. Instantly, she attempted to eliminate the inappropriate thoughts that vividly lingered in her mind. There was just something there she couldn't explain, until the funny feeling of somebody staring at her caused a quick glimpse over her shoulder. There she was standing seductively, eyeing Jessica with a splendid observation. "What the f——?" Jessica mumbled through a slight smile before she diverted her attention back to her friend. The pretty redbone stripper wasn't the type who liked to be disregarded as she approached, blatantly interposing Jessica and her company. They both trailed their lust-drawn attraction up and down each other. Jessica admired her luminous purple-cat-like contacts, glowing purple lipstick, and a glow-in-the-dark tongue ring, not to mention her thick thighs, wide hips, defined stomach, and perfect pair of breasts. Compared to Jessica, the woman appeared as a mythological female warrior. She stood strong and sexually intimidating in her five-inch black knee-high patent leather boots, black spider lace thongs, and matching spider lace top. Inflamed, she faced away from Jessica displaying her colorful ink that covered the back of her yellow skin, attractively all the way down to her plumb rear. Firmly, she pressed her body against Jessica, almost knocking her off-balance by the weight, and thrust her ass. She stood legs partially gaped and rhythmically gyrated her forty-two-inch hips into Jessica's midsection, causing Jessica's curiosity to whim boisterously as she captured the sexy gesture as an enkindling allurement.

The tantalizing exoticness urged the dancer to spread her legs farther and bend over craftily, bracing herself off the floor and then making her ass cheeks jerk rapidly. This was a scene Jessica would only observe usually through watching videos. It always seemed to intrigue her, the way they would move and utilize their bodies so effortlessly. Jessica giggled nervously, earnestly trying to elude the temptation only inches from her fingertips. Just as the idea came into existence, the dancer placed her hands on her knees and maintained Jessica's attention and bounced her ass in a fluent motion. Jessica was so mesmerized and completely turned on that she couldn't ignore the wetness that started to trickle down her thigh. "Oh my god," she mouthed.

Embarrassed she glanced toward her friends who all concealed the same sense of humor. Once Jessica regained her focus, all she saw was that thick, meaty yellow piece of flesh flopping recklessly to the beat, as Cardi B rocked the crowd. Finally, Jessica eased her highly manicured hands around the girl's slim waist and over the hump of her booty and cuffed a tight feel of the fluffy tush. She was in total ecstasy while she played with it, jiggling each cheek one by one, as if she was juggling hand to hand. The daring damsel looked back at her marvelous presentation, slowly extracting her long tongue and grazed it along her top lip. Jessica took to the gesture on demand, as everything around her suddenly became obsolete. She latched on to her ferociously and imitated a motion of f——ing her as she aggressively clashed her pelvis against her ass repeatedly. The dancer excitedly obliged to Jessica's playfulness and unknowing advance, grasping at her waist and tugging her along.

Jessica fraudulently dragged her feet while she strolled behind her with an exceeding smile, as the girl's curvaceous lower half moved irregularly from a bowlegged strut toward an entrance that was veiled with a black curtain. The deeper they got to the back of the club, the darker it seem to have gotten. Nevertheless, Jessica was on her toes, using her periphery to peep the shadows. She took notice of four other rooms with all the same overcast on its threshold, with strange sounds bearing from the other side. Once inside the room, Jessica entered casually, allowing the black drape to slowly fall at her back side, slightly reluctant. The dancer turned on her heels to face Jessica, easing a polite smile to her already pretty features.

Jessica's heart started to pulsate abnormally, but she was able to return the smile so genuinely. Before a word was even uttered from either woman, mysterious stranger progressed in her approach and passionately kissed Jessica on her sparkling lips. With just a slight touch of the tip of her tongue against the other, a moan ensued, and her hands greedily fumbled to unfasten Jessica's Gucci buckle, inserting her roaming hands inside the back of her snug-fitting jeans.

Gracing the fabric of her thong, she gripped her ass firmly, damn near lifting Jessica's 5'4" frame off the ground, her ass cheeks spread in the palm of her hand, as the warmth of her heat was felt upon the surface of her embrace. She easily directed Jessica's back up against the wall while she gingerly kissed and sucked on her neck, across her throat to be the other side of her neck. Jessica commenced to squirm a little under her pressure, but she was loving it, as she continuously announced her pleasure. The excitement was evident, the moment like a burning flame. They simply needed each other, and it was all seen in their touch and their urge. The dancer softly let Jessica descend from the wall and hastily disrobed her of every valuable article of clothing from her body, exposing a beautiful butterfly of a human underneath. She smelled of enriching lotions and oils. The dancer was on a heavy attack, as she began to finger f—— Jessica against the wall, pressing her breast sternly against Jessica's while she nibbled away at her flesh and adamantly worked her waist.

Jessica was now entering a different world, a state of pure bliss at every touch and kiss the girl would grant her, a place within herself she had never been before where she asked herself, "Girl, what are you doing? This ain't you." Yet she always wanted to explore the touch and feel of another woman. The desire of it all resulted in thick cum that slimed between the dancer's fingers. She retrieved her hand from Jessica's pussy and sucked the sticky substance off her own fingers, as Jessica's body slightly stiffened, her eyes faintly flickering and her knees lightly becoming weak. She exhaled a breath of relief while bracing herself against the wall. The dancer grinned devilishly before she went over to the black leather sectional sofa, sashaying through the small confines of a love seat, a vanity mirror, and a small table arranged with a few packs of condoms and a box of Philly blunts and a candy bowl filled with an assortment of peppermints and gummy bears. She reached underneath the piece of furniture, revealing a nine-inch black strap on. She walked back over to Jessica who's body appeared to be limp, and Jessica visually caught what the dancer had dangling from her grasp and instantly reframed her stance. Her pussy was soaked, cum stained her inner thigh like a piss stain, trailing off her skin like a sail, trickling as rain droplets streaming off glass. She tingled all over, tapping her foot fidgety, anxiously chewing on her fingernails.

"I want you to f—— me!" she said in a whisper. Squatting in front of Jessica, the dancer strapped the dildo around her waist and latched a piece underneath her pussy to stimulate her clit, the device fitting her like a thing. She stood back up while fondling Jessica's sudden protrusion to make sure it was sturdy enough for what she had in mind. She then leaned forward and wrapped her luscious lopes around the thick width of it, slowly causing her to emerge up and down, coating it with an abundance of saliva. Once it was nice and wet, she turned around, bent over, and braced herself off the armrest of the love seat, simply sliding her panties to the side.

Jessica in a timid manner approached her from behind, directing the head of it toward her pussy, but fumbling about trying to put it in. Eagerly the dancer reached underneath to assist with Jessica's faulty attempt. Excitedly she grabbed a hold of what she was in search of, easing the synthetic dick inside her, as she sort of crumbled. Jessica slowly pushed forward as the girl slightly moaned, adjusting herself to the fit. Jessica went deep as her pussy would allow her to. Then Jessica paused and extracted even slower.

"No!" the girl shouted over her shoulder. "Don't make love to me. F—— me!" she encouraged.

Jessica started to thrust inside her vaginal walls with such a force her ass clapped loudly against Jessica's region, causing the meaty aspect of the sexy dance to wave up on impact, a sight that truly entertained Jessica wildly.

*So this is what makes guys go bananas when they are f——ing a chick from the back*, she gleefully thought to herself. Jessica was so turned that she was now digging in her insistently. She gripped her shoulder, like how men do it, pulling the dancer more into her while her strokes became more pleasurable, more alluring. Her yells turned into a sharp, piercing plea, as they blissfully matched each other's.

"Yeeeeessss!" the dancer managed with her body being pounded mercilessly. Jessica unearthed her nerves of uncertainty. She lifted her hand and smacked her ass with each thrust. "Oh my god, yeeesss!"

she poured out behind each sting that sustained her juicy high yellow cheeks.

Jessica's pussy was throbbing endlessly, and she had the urge to cum again and again from the friction of the strap nestled against her clit. "Damn," Jessica uttered in a mild tone. Jessica embraced the control she possessed over the thick beauty, as she handled the girl aggressively, f——ing her exactly as she desired. Completely induced, Jessica pulled her hair, leaned over her sweaty back, and grinded inside her while she whispered in her ear. "Bitch, is this what you want?"

The girl was so caught up in the heat of the moment, she couldn't reply. The only thing audible was her modulated moans and heavy bursts of air. Jessica yanked her head back where her face grimaced. "Ooohhh." She uttered on some sh——.

"Bitch, you hear me talking to you!" Jessica said while still grinding inside her with a few short thrust.

"Yeesssss. Oh my god, yeesss, baby." She slightly struggled to announce.

The f——ing that was being put down was quite strenuous, and Jessica reclaimed her position, embedding her French tip fingernails into the woman's diminutive waistline. Jessica took full advantage of the situation and propelled herself into her body, completely knocking the girl off-balance and causing her to wobble foolishly in her stance. Something suddenly shifted within the room, instantly creating a disturbed sense as she lifted her head. She quickly caught a glimpse of a face in the mirror. She looked over her shoulder with a shameful expression, locking eyes with Daz Juan Costello.

# CHAPTER 7

Daz Juan and Jessica were sitting opposite of each other inside his impressive office space. It was an endearing space, eminent of a customized fish tank beneath their feet, covering the entire floor of exotic fish and baby sharks. Mahogany finished the walls, along with eighteen-carat gold trim and accents in the room of lavish comfort. Daz Juan couldn't conceal the goofy little smirk that spoiled his charm and handsomeness.

Jessica laughed. "What?"

Daz Juan simply just shook his head. "It's nothing, Ma." He tamed his playfulness. "So what's up, doe? What brought you here to my fine establishment?" He cockily leaned back in his chair.

"Well, I mean." She played sheep in her demeanor. "As you can see"—she made reference to the congested partygoers outside of the two-way mirror—"not only is it one of my friend's birthday celebration, but also it's a chance to pay homage to my guy." She smiled. "I haven't seen you since… Um." Jessica appeared to ponder. "Basically, since the wake of Fabian."

"Yeah, it has been a hot lil' second." His delivery was plain. Apparently he was giving Jessica the cold shoulder.

She surely took notice of his uncommon vibe through his disdainful behavior. "I see business is looking real good for you." Jessica scanned the rest of the office, observing a bunch of photographs of rappers and celebrities. A small tank of live lobsters sat idly in a corner next to a mini bar and grill. "Look at you, boy!" she convulsed excitedly. "I'm impressed."

"It's all in the grind, you know," he responded unboastfully. "It ain't nothing, doe." He sounded forbearing.

"F—— all this faking! Daz Juan, what's up?" Her tone was stern. "Do you have something you would like to bring to my attention?" she asked bluntly.

"Naw," he replied nonchalantly. "Not really. Why? What's up? What gave you that thought, yo?"

"Daz, I know you, and this isn't the Daz I know. Why you acting so strange?"

Jessica leaned forward placing her elbows on the pine oak desk and moving the basket of flavored French fries and a small platter of Wingstop spicy chicken wings, to demand his full concentration as she eased closer. Daz Juan was so earnestly willed to divert his stare more than he was willing to give it. Once he was caught in her hypnotizing gaze, the words she was expecting to hear emerged vexatiously from the tips of his tongue.

"You know the streets was buzzin' with your name after my boy Fabian was killed." Jessica gave him that look that seemed she was waiting for his next for sure line. "You, you was said to be the one who set Fabian up," he reluctantly finished.

"I heard that a few times before." She sighed. "Life will always come with accusations of something. People will consistently point their fingers and cast the blame on others for their own personal gain. Daz, it's not essentially how you view things, but what intersecting lines you see things from. Nothing is ever what it seems. Daz Juan, let me ask you something." An interval of silence occurred.

Daz Juan looked confused. "Asked me what?" His thick eyebrows arched suspiciously.

"What's your thoughts on the situation?" she inquired.

"My thoughts on what?" He appeared dumbfounded.

Jessica smacked her lips. "Really though. You going to sit over there and act like we just wasn't in conversation about something?" Frustration overwhelmed her tone. "You got to be kidding me." Her displeased expression caused Daz Juan to quickly forge a smirk upon his face.

"Naw. Chill, Ma. I'm just f——ing around. You, my bad. But look, at first I didn't know what to think actually. I considered myself to know you, just as much as you said you know me. So basically when it comes down to what you would do and won't do, I only know as much as you want me to know. You will never be truly capable of knowing a person as you expect to. Honestly, doe, I don't know how to think on that situation. So I never really gave it any thought." The lie was evident in the shift of his body, but it sounded good, convincing enough for him to even believe his own fabrication.

"That sounded inspiring, for a thought. Nice!" She nodded her head. "I see you been up on your studies, huh?" she spoke sarcastically. "'You will never be truly capable of knowing a person as you expect to,' Robert Greene, I assume."

Daz Juan peered over his shoulder glancing at the book *48 Laws of Power* on display as it was obsessively placed neatly next to the books *the Art of War* and *the 50th Law*. Daz Juan simply just smiled upon returning his stare into Jessica's looming gaze. "Naw, shorty. This ain't about me reciting any pages from a book. I'm just speaking the real. Noncipher. We just conversing, right?"

"Oh, no doubt!" instantly Jessica replied as she repeatedly nodded her head.

"But, hey, yo, excuse my rashness. What's up, doe Jess? I appreciate the love and all. You got Cardi B to rock the stage. That's what's up! That move enhanced the club's reputation fo' sure." He looked off momentarily, briefly hindering his words. "Yo, what you really here for?"

"You still got ties with your connect in China?" Jessica eagerly inquired.

Naturally Daz Juan eyed her strangely. "Ma, allow me to offer you something to drink. Where the f—— are my manners? Would you care for a glass of Amarone della Valpolicella Classico?" The syllables rolled off his tongue, spoken like a true Italian. He got up from his burgundy leather chair and strolled toward the mini bar. His stride was flawless, real smoothlike, and totally confident. His dark hair was spiked and slightly still curly with a nice tight fade. His skin glowed with such an ardor, along with the lingering irresistible power to please. He was well groomed from the whites of his teeth to his trimmed nose hairs and razor-sharp chin strap. Giorgio Armani scented his person as he moved about, looking dapper in his custom Italian menswear.

"No, thank you. I wouldn't." She sighed heavily. "So it's like that?" She tossed the question at his back. "I'm not a f——ing rat, Daz Juan. You ain't got to throw me off like I'm a lame or something," Jessica assured with hostility. "I'm not wired up." She stood up, stripping herself down to her bra and panties.

"C'mon now, all that isn't even necessary," Daz Juan insisted. He slowly inched his way back over to his seat with a glass catered in his hand. "Besides"—he sipped slowly—"you were already strip-searched." He chuckled.

"Damn! So it was like that," she responded while redressing herself, feeling mortified. "That was a slick little move." Mentally Jessica cussed herself out for allowing her curiosity to become a gesture of weakness.

"Just look at it from my position. I haven't seen you in years, and you just pop up at my spot. Ma, just a few years back, you were in federal custody on some other sh——. There's all kinds of things surrounding the mention of your name. And here you are now talking about connects. It's certain things you often don't speak on."

"Certain things as what? Please enlighten me," she replied cynically.

"Jess, you know the game just as much as I do." Daz Juan laughed.

"Apparently, I don't," she contested.

"All right, look!" he stated firmly. "I see where this possibly could lead up to. I'm not with all the back and forth sh——, especially when it's over something that makes complete sense. You, the daughter of an infamous drug lord, know that you don't pop up like a jack-in-the-box asking about any old cases and most importantly no connect talk," he explained casually.

"Yeah, but anyway." She waved off his last comment. "My reason in getting so ignorantly up in your business is because I'm simply trying to dump a nice load of coke on you for an excellent price," she said modestly.

Daz Juan stared with amusement. "Well, okay then." He eagerly rubbed his palms together. "Sometimes speaking numbers is the best language." He grinned. "What's on your mind, Ma?" He eased up in his seat.

"I like what you got going on here in Atlanta, honestly speaking. I'm trying to invest a little bit of my business sense into what you got going on."

"Like what, a partnership you mean?" Daz Juan looked baffled. "Yo, I don't play well with others. I'm all good by myself. Too many complications come with partners."

"I didn't really mean it like that. I'm just trying to leave my stamp in the A," Jessica responded.

"Huh?" Confusion read in his expression. "Jess, what you meaning?"

"As I said, I would like to offer you some grade-A cocaine straight from Sinaloa. You buy more than a hundred kilos, and I can guarantee you an undeniable deal."

"Yo." His index finger wagged relentlessly in her direction. "They said Fernando left your pretty lil' ass a nice piece of the pie. A hundred or more, huh?" He gradually nodded his head while massaging his chin. One could tell he was mingled with doubt by the deep wonder in his eyes. "You got them to go like that?" He brandished an appeasing smirk.

"Really questions are not needed for this conversation. Just like you said, sometimes speaking numbers is the best language," Jessica stated surely.

"I love your style," he replied. "Yo, let's say 3.4 mil."

A cunning smile eased upon Jessica's face. Her plan was to pipeline her narcotics from Mexico to Atlanta, utilizing Daz Juan and his crew to distribute her drug to all addicts and hustlers. Once Jessica is able to corner the market, where the streets will only depend on her product, then an astounding transformation shall occur. Jessica will effortlessly yet brilliantly create a hostile takeover, forcing Daz Juan into such a deplorable debt that he will have no other option but to forfeit the deed to his club, which would ultimately become a substantial drug hub for Jessica's organization.

Daz Juan's territory consisted of location, opportunity, and simply black book clientele that's worth an estimated 45 percent more than Jessica's Florida distribution—something she couldn't allow to slip through her delicate little fingers. Only if he really knew the game as much as he tried to make himself believe, if his vainglorious behavior didn't outweigh his common sense, then maybe he could take a peek of his opponent's game. Some things that people tend to force themselves to know are more than a mere page out of a book. Life's experiences can go further than knowledge itself. You must live life to obtain knowledge of it. Simply speaking, this was to be Daz Juan's first lesson in the gamble of the game. Never gamble anything you can't afford to lose.

"Um, 3.4," she rambled out loud. "$6,000 a brick, give or take." She calculated swiftly. "That's roughly about seven hundred keys." They both just looked at each other. Daz Juan's expression was emotionless. He didn't even blink. It was as if he was impaled on something. "Um, is that okay with you? Too much or no? Were you expecting to hear something else?" she inquired, doubtfully shaking her head and an added shrug of her shoulders, just for emphasis.

"Naw, my bad, yo." He smiled, allowing his body to relax. "Yeah, doe, it's all good, baby. In the back of my mind, I'm just avoiding the questions that might possibly screw this deal up for me."

"Oh no, not at all. What's your question?" Jessica proclaimed. "This is business, so negotiations are necessary."

"Jess, I'm just saying, Ma, what made you come to me with this proposition?"

"Two reasons." She displayed two fingers in the air. "One is because I knew you had the money and the drive to go through with it. Two, I'm looking to expand my reach," Jessica responded cocksure as her eyes roamed over the luxurious office that would soon be hers.

"How soon can we make this arrangement happen?" he asked with anticipation.

"I'm going to have my guy Julio link up with your guys. You still moving with the same crew, right?"

"No doubt!" He nodded his head in agreement.

"Okay, I know who to get in touch with. And after this conversation, we will never be on face-to-face basis again, unless it's absolutely a life-or-death situation. I'm a busy woman, and time is of the essence." She smiled adorably. "I will be sure to have someone trustworthy to introduce themselves to you on my behalf." Jessica stood up and extended her arm toward Daz Juan. "It was nice doing business with you."

"Likewise!" he said right as he accepted her soft hand into a firm shake.

"I'm so glad we were able to depart from each other with a better sense of understanding. Certain relationships should never be severed due to what other m———s have to say. I'm sorry about what happened to Fabian, but please know I didn't have anything to do with that. I was in love with Fabian. I would have never found any reason to cause him harm," she stated while batting long eyelashes repeatedly, confirming the tears that were slowly progressing in her eyes.

Jessica retrieved her hand from his grasp and quickly left the room with a nice switch to her voluptuous hips. Expectantly Daz Juan was certainly looking as he stimulated his bulging crotch, attracting little to no attention underneath his desk. Abruptly, the dancer that was lustfully caught up with Jessica in a sexual extravaganza appeared from an inconspicuous door hidden within the office. She approached Daz Juan's side, reached over his shoulder, and placed the loaded pearl handle chrome-polished .380 on the desk right in front of him.

"I seen right through that maggot-ass bitch," he spoke harshly.

"Now what?" she questioned, sneaking a gander at his rambunctious hand movement upon his lap.

"We wait," he replied. He smiled wickedly before looking up at the splendid young lady. "But, yo." He swung around in his chair, unbuckled his belt, and relieved his bulky nature from his trousers. She smiled back, but rather she smiled with ratification at the sight of his alluring erection. "Come, get on your knees for *Papi*," he demanded with the stroke of his dick.

She licked her lips. "Sure, Daddy." She eased between his thighs, and with no hands, she engulfed his dick all the way, until her tongue was tickling his scrotum. Daz Juan stared out the two-way mirror where he focused in on Jessica, as she joined in with her friends twerking on the dance floor. Daz Juan allowed his thoughts to fantasize about the notorious beauty, so much so he didn't even realize he was fiercely thrusting his dick down her throat, while he held her head firmly in place with both hands, until she started gagging and choking.

"Damn, shorty, my bad," he whispered, observing the ruin of her mascara tearing down her blush red complexion. He popped his dick from her mouth. He chuckled. She gasped, placing her hand to her chest.

"What the f——!" She cleared her throat and then smirked slightly as she looked up at him. She noticed his attention was elsewhere. "Damn, yo. She on your mind like that?" The girl regained her composure and trailed her tongue up the shaft of his semihard penis as it lay on his thigh, slowly raising it back to its peak of excellence.

Right as Daz Juan fixed his mouth to say whatever the first thing that came to his mind, the woman placed her finger to his dehydrated lips. "Shhhhh." She eased up fully. Standing in front of Daz Juan, interposed herself between him and the desk, she wheeled him a few inches backward. She untied the drawstring of her Under Armour sweatpants and pulled them down to her ankles. Then her panties dropped all the while maintaining eye contact, as Daz Juan anxiously engaged within his own touch. She stepped her Jordan out from her ruffle of clothing, turned around, spread her legs far apart, and bent over the desk.

"Come and f—— me like you want to f—— her," she instructed. With no indecisiveness, Daz Juan greatly obliged. Just as he put his dick in, he peered back toward the glass, coincidentally catching Jessica's gaze as if she was staring right at him. He was so excited he nearly cum off his fourth stroke.

# CHAPTER 8

Meanwhile, Julio arrived back in New York, only to be greeted by two FBI agents soon as he stepped off the private plane.

"Mr. Julio Ceaser?" one of the agents asked assertively.

Instantly Julio became startled after hearing his name being announced like that. Promptly he glanced over his shoulder, as he reached for the rear door of the tinted Lincoln MLK. He halted once he noticed the FBI shield they both brandished.

"Yeah, what's up?" he asked with an agitated expression. The two agents advanced closer. Julio shifted in his stance. He badly wanted to clutch for his pistol.

"I'm Agent Zelisko and my partner here is Agent Stowell. We would like to ask you a few questions."

"Ask me questions for what?" Julio spoke defensively. He eyed the two men with a strong sense of suspicion.

"Just come with us please. This shouldn't proceed no longer than twenty minutes," Agent Zelisko assured.

Julio didn't budge. He surveyed the area meticulously.

"We don't even have to leave the premise, no handcuffs. We're just here to talk," Agent Stowell added with a friendly smile.

Julio sighed before he paced toward them nervously. One agent led, as the other followed up the rear. They escorted Julio to a special interviewing room somewhere in the airport. Once inside the small box of a room, Julio maintained his tough guy demeanor, though he became weary, as the overwhelming number of murders he committed came to mind. Yet, the P95 Ruger concealed in his hip put him at an advantage. So politely he took a seat across from the emotionless middle-aged white men, who both maintained that stern, cop look.

"Y'all got me here. What's up?" Julio asked, looking from one to the other.

"What's up?" Agent Zelisko mocked. "Can you tell us why you left the state of New York without permission?"

"Huh?" Julio appeared dim-witted. "Permission!" He chuckled. "What's that 'pose to mean?"

"Mr. Ceaser, your federal papers stipulate you can't leave the state of New York without authorization from your PO," Agent Stowell answered.

Julio shrugged his shoulders indifferently. "Okay," he calmly said.

"So we have grounds to detain you," Agent Zelisko chimed in. "This means you will be looking at a violation. That's thirty-six months back in a federal pen."

"Again, what's up? Obviously, y'all want something. Quit with all the b—— and just spill it," Julio insisted with a lacking attitude.

The two agents glanced at each other before Agent Stowell retrieved a folder from his briefcase. "What does a cartel hitman have in common with a drug queenpin, a queenpin that's to be said at odds with your very own cartel?" Agent Stowell showed Julio the pictures of him and Jessica together at the meeting. Well, actually he showed photos of Julio exiting the motel, with Jessica doing the same moments later. He placed them neatly in front of Julio with a snobbish expression.

He laughed. "That's good photoshopping, because that ain't even me, and fo' sure I don't know who she is," Julio replied without glancing at the photos.

"Mr. Ceaser, you didn't look at the pictures," Agent Stowell said.

"You are telling us this isn't you?" Agent Zelisko intervened, firmly pressing his finger into the picture of Julio.

Julio simply just turned his head toward the wall, causing his thumbs to tap rhythmically on the table, tremendously annoying the two agents. "And you don't know Ms. Jessica McCray?" Agent Zelisko inquired with squinted eyes.

"Naw, man!" He turned back toward Agent Zelisko. "I'm trying to figure it out just as much as y'all."

The two agents couldn't keep their composure as they erupted into a hearty laughter. "You mean to tell me you don't have any ties to this woman?" Agent Stowell yelled, snatching the photo of Jessica from in front of Julio and holding it directly up to Julio's face.

"That's exactly what I'm saying," he responded with a grimace as he waved the 8 x 10 picture from his view. "Man, you buggin', yo!"

"Okay, allow me to try a different angle." Agent Stowell cleared his throat before adjusting his tie. "Let's talk about a Mr. Antonio Demarco."

"Who?" Julio sounded surprised suddenly.

Agent Zelisko pulled out his iPhone 8x from his jacket pocket. Julio's eyes was astonishedly transfixed once Agent Zelisko placed the phone in the middle of the table, where Julio noticed the play button on the screen. Instantly, Julio's fingers began to fumble nervously about in his lap. Agent Zelisko eagerly pressed the top of his finger to the screen, emitting Julio's voice to echo within the small confines of the room. The conversation between him and Antonio played intensely, the same conversation Julio utilized to get Antonio whacked. Slowly Julio reclined in his chair with a disheveled demeanor. He exhaled harshly as his heart sounded passively from his alarming chest. The agents got the reaction they were expecting, acknowledgment.

"You still sticking with your story?" Agent Stowell inquired with a greedy grin plastered on his face. After a few moment, Agent Zelisko palmed his phone and clicked a button, halting the recorded conversation into complete silence.

"You get the picture!" Agent Zelisko announced, placing his phone back in his pocket.

"I'm saying, am I under arrest or something?"

"No, not at this exact moment. You could be. That's all up to you. You can sit here and play 'the you don't know sh—— role' when it's evident you know more than what you are saying. Allow me to rephrase that." Agent Stowell smiled. "It's evident that we know more than what you are saying. That sound much better, right?" He looked toward Agent Zelisko, who just nodded his head calmly.

"Mr. Ceaser, you can make this real simple or make this real difficult," Agent Zelisko stated before he sat back ridiculing Julio's attitude. "I suggest you choose wisely."

"And what's considered to be simple?" was Julio's only sentiment.

"Well, for starters, what can you tell us about the whereabouts of Antonia Demarco?" Agent Stowell asked.

"Man, I don't know. Just because you got a conversation of me and this guy doesn't mean I know his every step."

"Yeah, but you flew all the way to Florida to meet with this guy, and now he's missing, a popular guy that hasn't been seen or heard. And here we have a man known to be accountable for over a dozen murders landing back in New York, who seemed to be the last person to see our CI alive." Agent Stowell twirled his pen between his fingers. "It certainly raises suspicion."

"CI?" Julio repeated, totally disregarding everything else that was said. He was baffled to be exact.

Agent Zelisko and Agent Stowell shared a quick glance. Agent Stowell knew he made a mistake. He decided to ignore it and keep the pressure on Julio. "This could be the homicide that can finally put you away for good. If Antonio Demarco's body is out there, you'll wish that wasn't a notch under your belt." Agent Stowell's stare pierced through Julio's faint reflection of his eyes.

"You got things all misconstrued," Julio declared. "He probably caught up f——ing on some lil' sleazy ass hoes or something."

"Oh, really." Agent Stowell chuckled. He looked toward his partner. "This guy thinks we are f——ing idiots." Agent Zelisko maintained his coolness, while Agent Stowell continued to grill Julio. "You and I both know Antonio Demarco isn't caught up f——ing on some lil' sleazy ass hoes. Now, where the f—— is the body?"

"Man, ain't no body," Julio replied annoyingly.

"I'm sure of that. We know how you cartel guys like to operate when it comes to getting rid of bodies. He's most likely chopped up in a million pieces dispersed in a pig farm somewhere or stuffed in a fifty-gallon drum full of acid or maybe even cemented into a new parking lot." Agent Stowell interlocked his fingers comfortably in front of him.

"Dude"—Julio snickered—"you watch way too many movies, my guy. That sh—— you assuming is some mob talk. This ain't the days of the good ol' American Mafia," Julio said logically.

"Thanks for the insight," Agent Zelisko spoke sarcastically as he leaned forward with a snarl on his face. "I'm tired of dancing around this bush with you. What makes you think even for a second we'll waste our time here questioning you if we didn't already know the answers? You think we got all this info from nowhere? Like we just making this sh—— up? You smarter than that. You been in one of these rooms on numerous occasions. And you surely know when the FBI is sitting across from you, it's deeper than your local PD. So let's stop playing the back and forth b——." Agent Zelisko relaxed back in his position, unflinching.

Julio just nodded his head and shrugged his drooping shoulders. His face frowned with attitude. One could sense he wanted to say something, but thought otherwise.

"Allow me to inform you on what we know so far." Agent Stowell eased back into the conversation.

"I'm listening," Julio replied.

"Murder for hire. But the ironic thing is the person that you were supposed to kill wasn't killed. Instead you and Ms. McCray are seen entering and exiting this motel with a slew of other members of her crew." Agent Stowell pointed to the sign of the motel in the pictures that read, "the Dolphin Inn," "Along with a few high-end vehicles that belong to Jessica and her crew. You see, a meeting of organized crime that was supposed to be arranged by a Mr. Antonio Demarco himself. Now, he has just vanished off the grid of all FBI surveillance. You see how all this is adding up?" Agent Stowell stood up from his seat and walked over to Julio's side, hiked up his slacks, and slowly placed his rear on the edge of the desk. "Do you understand how the disappearance of Mr. Demarco is pointing toward you?" he whispered.

"I see the picture you trying to paint. You can't allow your theory to be the reason for pointing your fingers at me. I don't have any idea of the whereabouts of Antonio Demarco. I don't have any knowledge of a murder for hire. Nowhere within that conversation is there anything discussed about me accepting payment to kill anybody, let alone anything mentioned about murder, period. I don't know what to tell you about this Jessica chick. I was just passing a face-to-face message under Los Zetas orders. That was my reason for going outside of New York. I was there for a day and gone the next. Man, that's all I can tell y'all," Julio stated with a lot of inspirational hand movements.

"A Los Zetas and a Jessica McCray in connection without any bloodshed." Agent Zeliska lifted his eyebrows, before he exhibited a sly grin. "Wow! That is so interesting. I wonder if your bosses are truly knowledgeable of you fraternizing with the enemy." Agent Zelisko laughed with a sinister tone.

Julio didn't find what he said funny. He knew that he was pinched, so he had to fold slightly just to get them off his ass. They had too much on him for all this to be just a simple shake of the bush.

"Man, what's up? What y'all want?" Julio was feeling the pressure. "I know of some Russians in Boston moving fentanyl by the bales."

# CHAPTER 9

The Lopez brothers and a few of their hooligans were huddled up in a stash house remotely in the sticks of Florida. Boxes of money cluttered the ruins of the enclosure. The smell of cigar, the stench of urine, and mildew lingered through the stagnated air. Within the bustle of currency being accumulated, three guys were lying facedown on the cockroach-infested wood board flooring, their ankles, mouth, and wrist duct-taped. One of the guys sustained a deep gash on the side of his bruised face from single blow from the butt of a pistol. The hot-tempered Lopez brothers paced back and forth, eagerly gripping identical gold-plated .45s, with fancy engravings in the palm of their hand. They both were rambling in Spanish. Meanwhile the other figures of their assemblage remained silent, standing attentive at the front door and a pair of continuously peeking through the ripped dingy sheets that partially covered the windows. They were armed with AK-47s strapped around their shoulders and Taliban-style turbans concealed their features.

"This f——ing bitch!" one of the brothers declared. "She thinks she outsmarted us."

"Calm," the other one insisted, placing his hand upon his chest. "Be calm, my brother. Patience is everything. Let's think rationally," he urged.

"I am thinking rationally. Where the f—— is the coke?" he yelled obnoxiously before inserting his boot in the rib of one of the guys on the floor.

"Easy, yo. We still accomplished something here. This is well over a million dollars, *si*?" The brother smiled, as his hands drew attention to the boxes of money and bundles of currency discarded aimlessly in the room.

"I want that bitch to suffer. Everything she hustled for, I want," he shouted belligerently. "I want her to lose sleep. She's out here thinking she's going to be the next Griselda Blanco. That bitch is sadly mistaken," the brother insisted. The hostility of him pointing his gun at the back of the skull of one of the fearful men at his feet instantly caused an impulsive reaction. He squeezed the trigger ever so happily. The loud bang was engulfing, muffling everyone's ears from the terrifying combustion. The other two men on the floor shook tremulously and whimpered helplessly as the specks of blood showered upon the man's skin next to him. Deliriously, the brother stood over his victim with the smoking barrel at his side. Craving to fire another shot, his long sweaty hair dangled over his distraught mug, a devilish and deceiving grin tediously emerging. His eyes shifted from the remaining two men, as if he was deciding which one he was going to kill next. His brother's hand suddenly eased on to his shoulder, distracting his thoughts. He turned to face his brother, obtaining a firm clasp on his shoulder, as he embraced the authorization in his brother's eyes.

"Hey, boss," one of the men standing guard at the door announced at a whisper.

Both the Lopez brothers looked at him with annoyance. "What?" the more high-strung brother said through clenched teeth.

"A UPS truck just pulled up, and there is a woman approaching the door with a big box," the man replied.

The brothers glanced at each other apprehensively.

"Okay, well, take that stuff off your face and answer the door," the brains of the two ordered. Soon as he said that, three soft knocks ensued.

The gun-toting man obliged and quickly displaced his weapon, before removing the fabric from around his face. Just then, the door swung open, and one of the brothers trained his attention toward the door, as an ungainly feeling settled in his gut. *A woman*, he thought. Then he had a flashback to the day when he witnessed Jessica disguised as a pizza delivery man take out the top boss Schivarelli. Immediately, he tackled his brother to the floor. Simultaneously as the brown box dropped from the woman's hands, a MAC-11 machine gun was revealed. The man's eyes widened with an intense fear. He wanted to run, but his feet were planted. His legs felt like lime and clay mixed with water and mortar. He was compelled to scream, yet he choked cowardly. Just before the horrifying sound abruptly erupted, six slugs ripped through his torso, lodging two additional bullets in his pelvis and three others tearing through the flesh on his thigh and hip, causing his limp body to crash awkwardly in the doorway.

Jessica continued firing, slowly stepping over the dead guy and passing the threshold while utilizing the weapon in a sweeping motion. Critically she gunned down another man as he attempted to flee toward the back of the house. Jessica was enraged as her finger was pressed on the trigger. In the midst of the bullets wildly flying, she noticed her intended targets crawling on their elbows and bellies while glass and pieces of plywood flew randomly. Greedily she enhanced a cherishing scowl. Removing her finger from the trigger, she enthusiastically aimed her weapon toward the brothers, but before she was able to entertain her thought, one of the armed men appeared from around the corner, the very same corner where his brains would be splattered all over the wall. With his AK-47 menacingly pointed in her direction, Jessica earnestly tried to reposition herself, but it was too late. The man hastily opened fire, hitting Jessica in her should, causing her to spin around and unfortunately drop her gun, as bullets dangerously whizzed by her. Panic overwhelmed her, as she bolted out the door, stumbling in the middle of the yard as blood seeped from her wound. Scrambling back to her feet, she rushed into the back of the truck. With much valor, the man advanced outside to get off a few more rounds, but seemingly his gun jammed. "F——!" he shouted. Struggling to clear the chamber, just as the live round ejected, five shooters emerged from the side of the house armed with AR-15s, M-16s, and MP5s. They ambushed the man with a barrage of bullets, before storming the house. Jessica was in a heap of hysteria. One of her men tried to calm her down, as he attempted to apply pressure to her wound.

"Jess, hey, chill." He forcefully held her down and ripped the shirt off her perspiring body. Unconsciously he eyed her breast momentarily. Using the shirt, he contained the blood slightly, but a 7.22-full-metal jacket upon flesh practically almost ruptured her petite frame. "Yo, cool. It went right through. Easy, doe. Breathe!" he instructed, preventing Jessica's provocation to panic and loss of consciousness. The heavily armed men moved impetuously toward the back of the exposed truck. Each man was speechless after seeing all the blood and noticing Jessica's quavering body.

"Man, she good?" one of the concerned men inquired sympathetically. Jessica nodded her head, before the man above her shot the other man a dismissing glare.

"Did y'all get them f———ing moronic, inbred bastards?" she coughed extremely as she moaned in agony, her face drawing back slightly. Silence sailed the air while everyone confusedly looked toward one another. "Answer me!" She mustered up enough energy to shout.

"Yo, they got away," a man's voice announced timidly from the group.

"What about our men inside?" she whispered.

"One dead, one injured, and one alive," another man replied.

"Leave them and burn the house into ash," Jessica said firmly.

"What about the money?" the same man asked.

"Did you hear me mention anything about any money?" Her tone became faint, her eyes fluttered lazily.

The man commenced to walk away along with the others.

"Arvonio!" Jessica called out. The man halted and glanced over his shoulder. "It's all counterfeit," she said. "Now, let's go. Get me out of here!"

# CHAPTER 10

Daz Juan woke up screaming and drenched in sweat. Another one of his dreams had manipulated his sense of harmony. He was breathing heavily, his heart beating abnormally, his eyes frantically swelled, shifting from wall to wall, corner to corner. The darkness played on his mind, while he tussled to free himself from the sheets that were intertwined with his body.

"Daz babe, it's all right. Shhhhh, relax, babe." The gentle voice consoled him while a tender touch caressed his back. Anxiously, he swung his feet out of bed, firmly placing them on the Persian rug. His greasy face rested exhaustedly in the palm of his hands. He sighed.

"Babe, here." She handed Daz Juan the tightly rolled Backwoods of popcorn kush, which slowly streamed a trail of smoke from her hand, as she impressively inhaled the tonic vapors. Momentarily he just looked at it a bit reluctant. Eventually, he accepted the polite gesture from the pinch of her fingertips and indulged in smoking the highly potent buds that contracted his lungs. He coughed hysterically. The woman got out of bed and strolled past Daz Juan completely naked heading toward the bathroom. Naturally, the enticement of her shapely figure caused him to give her a quick look over, before inhaling another cloud of smoke. He sat on the side of the bed thinking intently, his eyes staring bleakly at an idle pair of LeBron James Nike footwear sitting by the closet entry. After a few seconds, he heard the toilet flush, followed by a brief sound of flowing water from the sink. The woman returned to the bedroom in a pink terry cloth robe and sat right next to him, as she girlishly rested her head on his shoulder, before retrieving the brown leaf that dangled loosely from his lips.

"What's on your mind?" she questioned. "And please don't say it's nothing." She slowly toked.

"Man, I can't even call it exactly. I just got a lot in my mind," he replied weakly. "I guess, yo." He shrugged.

"Daz, stop it. It's that chick from the club, isn't it?"

"Yeah, something like that." He rubbed his eyes and then released a tedious yawn, before stretching his stiff limbs high above his head.

"Why are you allowing her to play on your mind like this?" the woman asked slightly bothered. "You giving the bitch way too much credit."

"You saying all that because you don't know what you talking about."

"I know enough."

"Apparently you don't, because if you did, you would understand the seriousness of this situation," Daz Juan insisted with a nebulous tone. "There's much more to that bitch than what meets the eye." He placed his hand on the back of her neck and gently gave her a tug. "Yo, baby, this thing can go sour real quick."

"Why? You said you were getting a better deal than what you are paying now, right?" she ashed the remainder of the blunt, before skimming her delicate touch across his sultry chest.

Daz Juan impeded her gracefulness and removed her hand courteously. "Indeed," he replied. "But everything that sounds so good doesn't always mean it is good. Sometimes in business, we deal with people not for the price, but because we know what to expect from them. I was always told you don't trust people who change like the season, but trust those who remain the same even when the season changed."

The woman nodded her head and smiled heavenly as if she was being enchanted by his words. "I just got a funny feeling about the whole proposition. After all these years, like all of sudden, now she wants to push these bricks on me." His voice was full of perplexity. "I just don't get it."

"Babe, everything will make sense." She kissed him ever so softly on his shoulder. "It always does." She moved her lips ardently toward his neck, tenderly tracing her fingertips along his bicep. "If you need me," she whispered, "just let me know. They say, if you f——ed once, you can f—— twice." She snickered only this time. "What a shame if Miss Lil' Pretty Thang to end up with her throat slit." She magically produced a razor blade on the tip of her tongue.

Daz Juan gave her an interesting look and flashed her a smile of admiration. "They don't call you Khari Blade for nothing." He laughed modestly. "Yo, you's crazy." He quickly resumed back to his abhorrent demeanor. "That actually don't sound like a bad idea." He became lost in his thoughts, thinking of the advantage he would have over the south if Jessica were dead. He would gain total control over the drug trade, as he always desired. "Take the head, and the body will fall." He considered to have thought.

"Exactly, babe," Khari Blade urged, only because she was fully aware of Daz Juan's affectation toward Jessica. Furthermore, she was becoming real territorial and simply obsessive over the thought of spending her life committed to him, which was a thought she felt compelled the moment she bent over his desk and told him to f—— her like how he wanted to f—— Jessica. Not only did he confirm her assumption, but also it was the best f—— of her young life.

"She certainly seemed like she was seriously into you." He nudged her jokingly. "And I didn't even know she f——ed around like that." He laughed remotely.

"What?" she appeared awestruck. "So what made you come up with that idea?"

"I was just shooting my shot. It is 2018. People are more comfortable in their own skin nowadays. People are more adventurous with their sexuality." He grinned. "But, yo"—he laughed—"I was onto something, doe. She was hitting your ass as if she really owned that dick. Low-key, I was in my feelings seeing that she was doing a better job with that synthetic joint compared to what I been working with between my legs for twenty-seven years." They both shared a genuine laugh.

"Babe, it's never a feeling like the real thing, them hefty balls smacking against my ass, that warm cum shooting all over my body." She moaned, guiding her hand into his lap and brushing nonchalantly across the tip of his dick. She smiled at the touch of his slight erection peeking through his Tom Ford boxers. Again, he removed her hand and placed it sternly on her exposed thigh.

Khari Blade smacked her lips with attitude. "Daz, what's wrong now?" she nagged.

"Pussy is not on my mind right now," he replied.

"I can't tell. Something is on your mid. Your dick over there seems to be thinking something different."

"My dick ain't nothing. I'm thinking on my toes." He reached for his cellphone on a small table stand next to the bed. "This Jessica chick is far from stupid. She moves with a purpose, and I got to find out what that purpose is," he said while flipping through his missed text messages.

"Okay, *Papi*. I understand. I'm parched." She stood up. "Would you like a soda or something?" She headed toward the bedroom entry, secretly mad as hell.

"Get me a bottled water, yo," he replied before she walked out of sight. "The flavored joint, peach, yo!" he yelled.

Her massive hips swayed down the lavish hall of Daz Juan Costello's customary home deep in a gated community in Atlanta's most prestigious neighborhoods. So distracted by her thoughts or just high off the kush, she never paid close attention to the oddness in her surroundings. Julio lingered in the shadows with an ice pick in his grasp. Khari Blade walked right past him, and just as she did, Julio advanced toward the bedroom, gingerly in step, constantly checking over his shoulder, making sure she didn't catch his sudden movement from her peripheral vision.

Julio entered the bedroom and approached Daz Juan as his head hung spiritless between his legs. Julio stood there until Daz Juan was able to feel his presence. When he looked up, he became startled once their eyes met and saw the point of the ice pick aimed directly toward his neck.

"Man, what the f——?" Daz Juan's hands were held dastardly in the air.

"Why the f—— did you make that deal?" His delivery was that of a whisper, but the aggression was evident. "Dude, what the f——

were you thinking, yo?" He knelt closer to his face. He said through clenched teeth, "3.4 million!"

"Man, actually she just caught me off guard. Yo, I wasn't expecting her to pop up on the kid. What's the odds in that, B?" Daz Juan reasoned with the same hushed tone.

"It don't matter. You could have easily dismissed that bitch and whatever she had to say. All you had to do was play the background and watch everything come together." Julio allowed his words to be sharply expressive, as specks of saliva landed absurdly in his face of fear. "Now, whatever you deemed possible, everything in what it was supposed to be could possibly come back on us, and you in here laid up with this scandalous bitch!" Julio's hand was firmly clasped around his throat.

Daz Juan struggled against Julio's unbelievable strength. "Yo, let me go!" Daz Juan urged, as Julio mumbled something indistinctively before releasing his harmful intent. "Calm the f——— down, B." He glanced behind Julio cautiously. "I'm confused, yo. What the f——— is you saying?"

"Man, listen!" He paced while he accumulated his thought. "Yo, the feds boxed the kid as soon as I touched JFK International."

"And you come here to my residence."

"Yo, I ain't hitched, dude." He lifted his shirt. "Bruh, your name never came up. They was just asking mad questions about me and Jessica. That ain't even why I'm here yo," Julio confirmed.

"Please, explain why you are standing in my bedroom with an ice pick to my neck," Daz Juan pleaded.

"The body of Devecchio washed up behind Jessica's house," Julio responded infuriated. The look in his eyes was penetrating. He was unflinching as he stood over Daz Juan with much domination. Daz Juan was muddled. He shook his head. "Naw, allow me to rephrase that. The body you were responsible disposing of."

"Yo, that's impossible," Daz Juan uttered.

"But it's not!" Julio insisted.

"I made sure my guys took care of that correctly and inconspicuously," Daz Juan replied matter-of-factly.

"Well, I'm telling you differently. With that being said, Jessica is digging way too much into it. She's mad determined, yo. Bruh, if she finds out the link between Devecchio and us, then she going to unearth the truth of our entire motive."

Daz Juan nodded his head. He exhaled. "What's Antonio's thoughts on it?" he questioned with concern filling his tone.

"F——, dude. He's dead," Julio said out of spite.

"Dead?" Daz Juan repeated.

"Jess killed him." Julio lied.

"Huh? For what?"

"Man, stop with all the questions. Antonio knew too much anyway. We needed him dead. Now, it's just Jessica and us knocking her off her pedestal and seizing her position. My superior wants her head and, in exchange, we gain control of her distribution. We'll gain access to the tunnels in Mexico, not to mention $2 billion worth of Sinaloa's product. We'll be able to put a grip on Detroit, Cincinnati, and Columbus, Ohio, and cities farther east. We good, fam." Julio quickly eased off to the cut as he heard Khari Blade at a short distance.

"Babe, here you go." She handed Daz Juan the cold beverage of his request. "Guess what just flashed across the TV screen as breaking news?" Daz Juan cracked the seal and took a swig. Khari Blade continued, "They said mob boss Whitey Bulger was beat to death in his cell, and they even attempted to cut out his tongue. A mafia hitman was behind the attack," she gloated.

"That's what happens when you volunteer information of notorious gangsters to the feds," Daz Juan replied. Yet he couldn't help but think about what Julio had just said with all his fast-talk gibberish. He realized he really didn't need Julio, but Julio needed him. Daz Juan knew he was the ultimate hustler. And Julio was nothing but a goon. Daz Juan could easily have Khari Blade murder Julio and Jessica and simply remain firm in his stance.

"I'm about to take a quick shower. You good?" she said, stalled at the threshold, clearly hinting that he come and join her with a smirk and mere exposure of her cleavage.

"Yo, I'm good, Ma," he replied insincerely.

"Well, if you need anything," she teased, "and I mean anything." Khari Blade allowed her robe to fall to her feet. "Don't be a stranger." Slowly the door closed, and as soon as it did, Julio reappeared like a ghost.

"I just don't want you to decide at the last minute. That bitch won you over with a sense of fraudulent flattery. Yo, a lot of sacrifices were made in order for us to even get to this point. Backing out isn't even an option, fam," Julio earnestly stated further.

"Nah, yo, it ain't never nothing like that. I know exactly what's all on the line here. You just hot, B. What we don't need is any unnecessary heat, yo," Daz Juan stressed.

He didn't trust Julio. He just tolerated him due to his cartel connections and the fact Antonio Demarco talked so highly of him. Daz Juan just never seemed to embrace that mutual prospect of the guy. Julio was too slimy for Daz Juan's taste.

Daz Juan, Fabian, and Antonio Demarco were all a tight ingenious trio of ambitious adolescents. The legacy of their fathers is what held them equally. Although their common ground emerged from different walks of life, they all had the same agenda and shared the same scrapes and bruises. They strived for that same respect, that same urgency of power and wealth. Now, Daz Juan sat facing the man who he knew killed Antonio Demarco, just as he always assumed Julio of murdering Fabian, and of course he would cast the blame on Jessica.

True, Jessica was a grimy bitch, and Daz Juan knew of her affair with Antonio and Fabian and without a doubt everything she stood to gain with both of them dead. So he believed her word played a major role in the killings, but Julio was actually the *killer*. Playing both sides of the fence, it was no longer chess, but rather cutthroat. Daz Juan stood up facing Julio.

"Besides, who declines an offer of six thousand a brick? You know what I can do with seven hundred bricks, yo?" Daz Juan continued.

"So she told you six thousand a brick?" Daz Juan nodded his head before taking another gulp of water. "But, yo, that's well over

3.4 mil. To be exact, 4.9 a brick sounds more reasonable. You making out a million and some change just on the pay out."

Daz Juan shrugged his shoulders. "Fam, I'm great at math and even better at business, so tossing all these numbers around for what, yo?"

"You got to think of why. Is what you should ask yourself, B. I never known a murderous drug lord such as Jessica to be so generous. It's not her style, yo."

Daz Juan appeared dumbfounded. As much as he didn't want to, he had to admit Julio had a point.

"But I get it, doe, long as you got it figured out. Man, we got bigger things to occupy our mental space with, like this f——ing boy situation. Yo, we got to clean this sh—— up," Julio wisely suggested.

"So what's up? What do we do?" Daz Juan expressed.

Julio snickered. "Bruh, it ain't about what we"—he pointed his finger back and forth between himself and Daz Juan—"going to do, because we didn't make this into a situation. You did!" Julio thrust his finger into his chest.

"At least tell me where the body is," Daz Juan insisted vexatiously.

Julio looked at him foolishly. "Yo, you kidding, right?"

Julio's and Daz Juan's eyes quickly darted toward the bathroom door once they heard the shower cut off. "You need to be trying to make sure that Devecchio m—— didn't leak all the wrong things to all the right people."

Julio slowly walked backward. "Yo, D, be loyal to those who are loyal to you, not to those you fear. Being a fearful man will only get you killed." He smiled. "Yo, I hate to be the one to kill that guy, since my lil' sis had a crush on you." Julio left his words hanging in Daz Juan's mind, as he turned around and calmly vanished. No sooner after he left, the bathroom door opened, emitting a dim light into the bedroom.

Khari Blade flirtatiously emerged from the condensed water vapors. Her body was wet, as she stood graphically trying to capture Daz Juan's attention. Daz Juan's hand balled into a tight fist. He stared languorous into the emptiness of where Julio once stood. She called his name repeatedly. He continuously just stared, not even a blink nor recognition of the beautiful curves tempting to entice any man's desire. Khari Blade frowned, again flustered with emotion, before stepping back and slamming the door.

# CHAPTER 11

"I just know your profession, your true profession, that is, you have been a loyal asset to a lot of guys I know, either personally or just through business. Ironically, when I need certain things handled that necessarily won't bring my cartel any heat, your name seem to always come within earshot. Hell, they even considered you the best, since the legendary iceman."

Detective Winsten remained silent and seated while being watched strenuously by four armed gunmen. Sternly he was questioned by the feared cartel boss who ominously stood before him, a diminutive man with a large ego.

"I suppose, so I said to myself, if my sons were to come up one day—let's just say missing without a trace, no ransom, no crime scene, no nothing—the question came mind was, who would have the capability to do that?" He grinned. "And guess what the answer was?" He looked to the detective.

The room was quiet, motionless even. Detective Winsten appeared disinclined, thinking if it was a formal question really intended for his response. "No, no, my friend. Please, speak." The boss seemed to have read into his hesitation. His hands were casually confined inside the pockets of his slacks, while he rocked back and forth eagerly off the heels of his soles.

"I guess me, or else I wouldn't be spending my Saturday morning with strange men armed with military-style assault rifles invading my home," the detective replied.

All the men in the room exchanged a slew of different expressions. Unexpectedly, everybody in the room erupted into heavy laughter, all of course except Detective Winsten. In fact, he was emotionally tensed, unaware of what the maleficent humor was related to. He became fidgety.

"Well, yes, my friend." He quickly dismissed the amusement from his features. "My next question is, do you have any knowledge of my sons' whereabouts? Now, before you respond to that question, I want you to understand I'm only going to ask you one time. If I find out you are not being truthful, I will personally erase your entire bloodline and leave you to mourn their loss, but eventually I will kill you as well. Do we agree?" His tone was definite.

He stepped in short paces. His $3,000 reptilian boots reflected with a heavy gloss, as the sun's radiant energy peeked through the sheer curtains in the place Detective Winsten would usually consider his place of devotion, far away from the city noise, annoyance, and simply any unwanted traffic of humanity. It was an uncommon place to be, if one took the time. The effort in its arrival seemed almost impossible. The brush was thick, with a long, winding dirt road leading discreetly toward his home. His backyard was a site destined for nature analysis, as wild cats roamed artistically through the dense trees, snakes slithered and coiled, and small lizards scampered abundantly. Never did he think waking up to a freshly brewed pot of coffee, a splash of hazelnut, and four sugars would amount to this, a face-to-face with the man known in the FBI's most wanted list as Luca Gussalli.

"I don't have any inkling of where your sons are, Mr. Gussalli. I'm not even aware of that particular incident. This is all new to me," the detective declared wholeheartedly.

"Detective"—Gussalli glared—"you mean to tell me you weren't ordered to make a pick up at 3376 West Palm Beach?" He viciously eyed the jittery detective.

"West Palm Beach," he mumbled incoherently. He looked toward the shiny stone that layered the floor beneath his calloused feet. He seemed to be in a daze of disorder. He continuously repeated the address at a low mumble, forcing a false impression that he didn't know what Gussalli was talking about. "I can honestly say I don't recall anything happening in or around West Palm Beach," the detective finally spoke assertively.

"Please, Detective,"—he stepped closer—"don't tell me something you might think I want to hear. Tell me what you know I need to hear." Gussalli reached over to one of his men and retrieved a chrome .357 revolver from its holster, showcased on the hip of his Levi's jeans. Gussalli allowed his gold-and-diamond-embellished finger to rest on the trigger, cocking the hammer with the pull of his thumb.

"It's obvious that I'm picking your brain, Detective. The only reason I'm entertaining these f——ing lies is on behalf of my sons' whereabouts," Gussalli stated coldly.

Detective Winsten stalled while staring fearfully at the right hand of Gussalli that clutched the hefty revolver. In the midst of the detective's thoughts, he knew if this man really had any knowledge of his involvement, his head would have been stuffed in a guillotine.

"Mr. Gussalli, I'm going to keep saying the same thing. I don't have any clue about anything you are referring to. I'm sorry to hear about your unfortunate situation, but this right here is beyond everything I stand for, which I'm sure might sound ridiculous. Mr. Gussalli, I'm no idiot," he persuasively assured.

"Detective Kevin Winsten"—Gussalli chuckled—"you disappoint me. My expectations of you were much higher. It's so amazing how people don't seem to cherish life, how simpleminded people can often be, all behind circumstantial words." He shook his head. "Incredible," Gussalli added. "I know for a fact Jessica McCray called you to remove my sons and clean up the scene, as she had all these years. All I want is their remains, Detective, and possibly you'll be able to walk away from this situation completely unscathed." He smirked.

"I can't produce something I don't have any knowledge of," he yelled unexpectedly. "Gussalli, I'm telling you I don't know what you are talking about, honestly," he said behind a heap of emotions.

"I doubt that, Detective." Gussalli placed the barrel of the .357 between his eyes. The hard steel was forcefully pressed against his forehead, causing Detective Winsten to become a bit apprehensive. His shoulders were tightly tensed.

"Please, Mr. Gussalli. That's not necessary. I'm right here. I get the point." He attempted to swipe the gun away from his face, but suddenly the detective felt massive arms looped around his neck forming an unyielding squeeze on his throat. Instantly, the detective commenced to express a sense of fright. He squirmed endlessly, his hands desperately clawing at his attacker, fighting his urgency to draw air into his lungs.

The boss laughed hysterically before shouting, "Enough!" The man released his gripped and slowly backed away. "You are in no position to tell me what's not necessary." Gussalli again pressed the gun firmly to the center of the detective's forehead. "I need you to understand this is only the beginning to what you can expect from me. Until I give my sons the proper burial they deserve, I'll be sure to make your existence a living hell."

He motioned to one of his guys. Entering the living room with a sheet swathed around her fragile body was a young girl with tears spilling from her swollen eyes. An AR-15 muzzle was directed toward the back of her skull, as she was ushered by a man with a ski mask, concealing his features. He pushed the girl effortlessly to the floor. A slight whimpered eased from her mouth, as she nervously removed a few strings of brunette hair from her sight.

"Pleeeassseee!" she pleaded and sniffled. "Let me go. I promise I won't say anything. I swear!" She looked up to the men who hovered over her with an eerie impression of bloodlust in their eyes, like a pack of hungry wolves.

"You like them young, Mr. Winsten, I see." Gussalli peered at the helpless girl. "She can't be no older than sixteen," he spoke to his accompanying attendants, before he frowned at the detective. "This can't be your daughter, because then comes the question, Why would a daughter sleeping in her father's bed naked?" He laughed. "But we all know the answer to that. Little girl, how old are you?" Gussalli knelt beside her.

"Fifteen," she innocently whispered.

"Wow! You don't say. Fifteen years young." He trained his attention back on the detective, who appeared soaked in sympathy, as he struggled not to look at her. Gussalli shook his head with disgust.

"What is it that you won't do? But then why bother even trying to find logic in a person with no morals, am I right?" Gussalli grinned. "None of us here are saints, so who am I to judge?"

He simply nodded his head and turned his back, whistling lightly. A loud thunderous sound exploded, which caused the detective to jolt in his seat. Quickly, Gussalli spun around on the heels of his boots, examining the litter of brain tissue all across the floor. The burst of blood speckled the detective's feet and decorated his cargo shorts. Gussalli trailed his finger through the thick pool of serum that slowly started to develop around her head and sucked the substance off his finger insanely. "Yeesss!" he shouted absurdly. "You see, Mr. Winsten, that's what makes for a nice hard erection." Gussalli groped at his penis. Tossed his head back and screamed.

The room fell to a deafening halt. Gussalli paused, staring at the ceiling oddly. A chilling cringe spiked the detective's spine. Gussalli suddenly expressed a wicked gleam, as he seemed to have gloated over the lifeless young girl. Detective Winsten appeared devastated. Once again, the two men exchanged glances.

"Lead me to my sons, Detective. Jessica McCray is nothing but a curse. Don't allow her to be the death of you," were his last words, before the group of guys nonchalantly headed toward the front door.

Once the thick layer of oakwood parted from its structure, it was as if a sense of relief breezed through, like a rushing force. The freshness of outside impetuously overwhelmed the detective, like a whistling flurry. He finally looked at the girl. *Such an aspiring and beautiful young woman she was*, he thought to himself, as he choked up momentarily, though he couldn't catch the salty fluid that trickled from between the lashes of his eye. The powerful caliber imploded a huge hole in the back of her head, creating an even larger one that exited through her forehead. Her emerald-colored eyes were fixed in a helpless terror. Her once pale complexion was now defined with much gore. Blood slowly outlined the detective bare toes, as the warmth of its substance had a tingling sensation crinkling his flesh. He was mortified. He felt guilty, shameful even. Despite the ridicule and age difference, Detective Winsten allowed his heart to embrace the girl as the love of his life. Weird as it sound and completely iniquitous it was, the detective accepted the notion, "Life being what you make it out to be." Love isn't about age, but it flourishes through action.

Hate began to brew in his heart, just the same as the rage that was building in his veins.

# CHAPTER 12

Khari Blade was in Columbus, Ohio, trailing a white 2018 Toyota Camry, which was equipped with various hidden compartments that hauled massive amounts of contraband. This particular haul contained twenty pounds of Sour Apple diesel, twenty kilograms of heroin, and fifteen illegal fully automatic assault rifles. They exited the freeway on Seventeenth Avenue. Khari felt excited to be back in the city she so fervently used to call home, bringing her black-on-black Range Rover and Toyota.

Instantly Khari became rattled with nervousness, as she had no option but to follow through with her turn. "Oh sh——," she murmured. Slyly she retrieved her full auto Russian TEC-9 from the passenger seat. She gripped it firmly. Rolling her tinted window all the way down, her finger was pressed gently against the trigger, her heart racing. Approaching Cleveland Avenue, the light turned red, causing Khari's chest to strike repeatedly. Coming to a complete stop, she checked her rearview mirror, as the seconds tediously ticked away.

"Man, what the f——!" Khari began to grow impatient, relentlessly tapping her fingernails against her steering wheel. Just then the light turned green, and simultaneously the highway patrol car's taillight flashed, indicating a right turn. Khari sighed heavily, just before releasing the built-up tension in her body. She allowed a slight smile to crease the side of her mouth. She placed the TEC-9 back on the passenger seat and turned up Moneybagg Yo's song, slightly vibrating through the car speakers.

Crossing Cleveland Avenue, the Toyota was already turning the corner of Brooks Street, and Khari kept forward, before easing to the curb of her grandmother's old house, where her little brother and a few of his friends stood attentively.

Her brother casually approached the vehicle. "What up, lil' bruh?" she said ecstatically, as the passenger window slowly unveiled Khari's vigorous smile and warm features.

"What's up, Hollywood?" He laughed bashfully.

Khari smacked her lips. "Damn! It's like that?" she replied, though she still maintained her zealousness.

"Naw, I'm just talkin' sh——." He snickered. He leaned inside the SUV and slapped hands with his sister.

"Oh my god, you tall as f——." She laughed hysterically. "What? You like GI?"

"Something like that." He grinned.

"That's what sixteen look like? Wow. F—— all this street sh——. You need to be striving for a basketball scholarship," Khari said. Her brother simply just turned his head. "You still in school, right?" Her tone shifted. Her brother was reluctant to speak. He just stepped back a few feet, as he looked tensely up and down the block. "Decarlo!" she shouted. He glimpsed in her direction. "Nigga, you better step back over to this m—— vehicle," Khari demanded. "I don't know what you think this is. I don't know if you trying to impress your homeboys or what. But I'll get out this bitch and beat your m—— ass."

Decarlo knew his sister all too well to be calling her bluff. "Man, I'm saying, sis," he covered their distance with a long stride. "I got a lot going on out here. I'm trying to maintain this hustle and maintain my sanity from killing one of these niggas," Decarlo insisted.

"F—— that!" Khari spoke out angrily. "All that sh—— sound like excuses. All you need to maintain is the movement. I supply the product, and you coach the team. The whole purpose in being a leader is to lead, so f——ing lead!" Khari had a short fuse. She leaned back, slouching in her leather seat, and held her hand on her forehead, feeling annoyed. "Hey, D, we simply agreed you stay in school, which you said that you understood it wasn't always about the flip, but—" Khari allowed her head to roll lazily toward him, as she awaited his response.

"A stepping stone for what is yet to come and then you said to hustle simply means to work strategically toward success when the odds are against you." Decarlo smiled at his fuming sister.

As hard as she attempted to come off, she couldn't ignore the fact that she missed her family. Khari returned the gesture ever so pleasantly. "That lil' charm might work on these hoes out in the streets. But I'm your sister, and that sh—— ain't about to fly." She slightly laughed.

"C'mon, sis, lighten up." He reached his long arm through the window and nudged her knee. "Chill." He continuously smiled.

"I'm saying, D, big bruh is on his way home. Promises were made on everybody's end. We got obligations out here, D. Well, you were a baby when bruh got knocked, and y'all's bond was only built through penitentiary visitations, letters, and phone calls. But you know who you brother is and what he stand for." Decarlo magnetically seized his sister's eye contact, as she spoke. He sincerely nodded his head. "You might not see it as such or probably still a lil' wet behind the ears, but we owe it to bruh for him to come home and reclaim his throne. He been gone for fifteen years, and his presence is still held firm amongst us all. The last thing I need is for you to fumble at this point," Khari continued.

"Okay, sis, you right. I get what you saying. I'll go back to school. That sh—— just be so f——ing boring. Everything I need to know I'm learning out here," Decarlo responded.

"I understand all that. Trust me! But these streets ain't worth the dedication. It just look good. To win is to have something to show for yourself in the face of society, and it's certainly not about the flash of this sh——. But to sit back and make it easy for your grandkids, to be that voice when you're old and wrinkled, to still be heard as a voice of wisdom," Khari spoke wisely, just before she observed Decarlo's eyes trail off.

Kevin Gates's "Luca Brasi 3" played modestly from a slow passing tan sedan. Its tinted windows were slightly open, just enough for the strong stench of marijuana to be expelled heedlessly by the occupants inside. Khari squirmed in her seat to see what actually caught her brother's eye. It wasn't a car of familiarity, but its big fancy chrome rims stood out to Khari as just a typical street cat, she assumed. Unexpectedly, the sedan made an aggressive maneuver by cutting right in front of her and bringing the car to an abrupt halt. Khari's acquired tendency caused her to react again, only to come up short, once Decarlo interjected her move by the clasp of her tiny wrist. Khari was taken by surprise, quickly reacting with a daring glance toward Decarlo.

"Relax, sis. That's just Po," her brother announced with a smirk. "My niggas on point out here."

Before Khari could respond, a tall lanky figure appeared from the back seat of the vehicle, dressed plainly in a blacked-out Buckeye football jersey and a pair of gray sweats, ruffled over the tongue of his gray suede Timberlands. The evening committed his features to be obscure, besides the diamonds that reflected brightly off his neck, forming ridiculously into an immense emblem that rested at the center of his chest. He was sluggish in his walk, as he appeared close. He was dark-skinned with wavy short hair. His mouth was a cluster of canary stones set in a platinum. His vocabulary seemed to have glittered with every verb and a noun, as he casually jived with the youngers that stooged in the gloom of the night. Khari's dazzling eyes were attached to his every move, even mesmerized by his rugged hood swagger.

Eventually Po diverted his attention over toward Decarlo. He peered with his eyes partly closed. Despite his euphoria from his induced high, he squinted curiously inside the Range Rover. Catching Khari's distinguishing appearance, Po smiled in full animation. Seeing Po's hastened approach, Khari became jittery, as she attempted to conceal the excitement that overwhelmed her.

"Dio, what up?" He tossed his arm across the back of Decarlo's neck. "Who we got here?" he questioned jokingly.

Khari blushed, while Po and Decarlo just smiled mischievously. Not only was Po Khari's big brother's right-hand man, but also he was her ex-lover and the one she secretly lost her virginity to. Just like her big brother, Po was a murderer. Rumor has it Po accumulated over a hundred contract killings in his name, *allegedly*. Nonetheless, Khari knew unquestionably that Po was indeed a killer. She bore witness to her big brother's and Po's insidious actions at a young age. That was a moment in her life when she was nothing more but vulnerable and such a doltish teenager, who chased a reckless young boy. Khari was attracted ultimately beyond his considerable good looks and amazing charm.

"Boy, stop." Khari snickered. "It ain't been that long." She grinned.

"The last time I seen you, you was shaking your ass in a Gucci man video, which was looking real juicy, I may add." Po and Khari exchanged a passionate sense of energy within their stare. Decarlo picked up on the vibe and slowly eased out of earshot, as he commenced to fraternizing with his lingering cronies. "What's good, doe? What brought your sexy self back to the hood?"

"Damn! Just because a bitch advanced past the stigma of being stagnant to one block as if this is it when there's a whole world to explore outside of this hood sh—— doesn't mean I forget where I came from. I'm still hood as it gets. I'm just thuggin' my sh—— on a different scale. Please, don't get it confused." Khari cut her eyes into a straight attitude.

"Hold tight, killa'." Po chuckled. "Baby, I was just being cordial," he added. "You is too cute to be sitting over there with your face all frowned up. I can't get a hug, a kiss, or something?" Po urged joyously.

Khari couldn't contain her enthusiasm. Before she could actually respond, Po was already leaning his body halfway through the window. Khari felt the underlying pressure from Po's vigorous personality. Then he graced her thigh with his willful need to touch her. A deep continuous sound rolled from her throat. She closed her eyes, as Khari slowly inched toward him, allowing her lips to press gently against his, ever so fervently. Their lips slightly parted, and the tip of their tongues engaged in a blissful exchange. Khari struggled to refrain her mouth from devouring Po's entire face. She pulled away and simply just savor with amusement.

"Thanks for everything, Po," Khari spoke softly while caressing his nearly well-proportioned beard.

Retrieving back to his originality, perplexity disturbed his once meritorious expression. "Huh? For what?" he marveled.

"Just for you being you, for being that guy I always expect you to be." Khari gazed at Po, right as he licked his succulent lips. A slight tingle surged between her thighs. The mere thought of Po's face nestled within her pussy was so intoxicating. Po's eyes seemed to have brighten, curving the corners of his mouth upward. He beamed, as if he could read her mind, or if he had the same thing in mind. Abashment settled unexpectedly.

Quickly, Khari recovered from her embarrassment. "Well, anyway what brought me back to the hood"—she laughed in a partly stifled way—"is to see my lil' brother and to see how things are transpiring out here."

"You know we standing firm, holding it down. We got Cleveland Avenue under lock and key from Eleventh all the way up to I-61." Khari nodded her head, as she retained what Po was saying to her. "Everything is smooth, K. No worries. Big bruh going to be proud of lil' sis," he spoke sincerely. "I almost forgot. I end up finding two buildings for lease on Morse Road that look to be good prospects for that strip club and seafood restaurant big bruh had mentioned," Po added while looking around his surroundings. He was just being vigilant toward the vast movement that suddenly emerged behind him.

"Excellent!" Khari rejoiced. "Now, this is where we get ready to switch lanes." She smiled honorably. "Get with the business lawyer and get that lease signed and documented immediately. Get with the bank and have them fax me a bank statement and credit report," Khari declared. Po agreeably nodded. "I'm going to show y'all how to reverse drug money into hard-earned money that can't be confiscated."

"That's cool, baby, but I need you to keep in mind everybody don't have that option. For most of us, ain't that easy. Life gives us all different challenges," Po replied.

"True story, but you must strive for change. You got to want to better yourself, a better living. Life will only give you what you are willing to accept from it. Po, there's so much more to this lifestyle than what you are allowing yourself to recognize. There is no point in playing the streets if you can't protect your assets. See what I'm saying? Po, you need to obtain a purpose, bro, straight up," Khari explained.

"Real talk, doe," Po responded quickly. "I like the sound of that. I can't even front. You know your boi live for this hood sh——." He laughed, as he reached his arm through the window, matching palms with Khari. "But I also live for anything that make sense." Their hands interlocked with such a strong desire. "K, I'm ready to boss up. Imma follow your lead. Let's get it!" Po was triumphant.

Khari brought forth a devious grin. "I'm so glad to hear you say that." A rambunctious killer such as Po was exactly who she needed as one of her puppets. "Hey, remember that New York thing my pops had you and my brother do?" she asked meekly.

Po simply nodded his head, giving Khari a suspicious eye. Khari certainly picked up on it and couldn't conceal her amusement. She giggled, before saying, "Nigga, you think I'm trying to dateline you or something?" This caused Po to leap forward with laughter.

"Naw, baby, it ain't like that. Just a natural reaction." Po chuckled. "But what about it, doe?"

"So you remember the daughter that was said to inherit her father's drug empire, right? Well, actually the empire my pops thought he was entitled to," Khari continued.

"Yeah, yeah, of course. What about her?" Po sounded anxious.

"I finally made contact with her, and when I say she is connected on a major scale, I mean that literally." Po fiddled with his beard, appearing to be in deep contemplation. "Put your mind to it and let me know the first thought that pops up."

"What your crazy-ass pops got to say about it?" Po curiously inquired.

"He has nothing to say about it, because there's nothing for him to know about," Khari answered surely.

"And what about ABL? Isn't this something we should bring his attention?" Po questioned.

"Which we will, accordingly, that is. I guess he going down to Florida day one to see his lil' model chick. We going to let him get that fifteen years of tension out of his system before we bring any type of business conversation to his attention. So right now, this is just between me and you," Khari advised.

"Fo' sure. Fo' sure," Po assured. "But what makes you think your pops won't find out, considering whatever thought we might decide to entertain? Dude is not only a lunatic but also a f——ng homicide detective."

# CHAPTER 13

Back in Florida, approximately four o'clock in the afternoon, the Lopez brothers bravely lingered in one of Jessica's high-end saloons. One of the brothers kept constant watch out the window toward the parking lot and the commotion of pedestrians. The aroma of whiskey reeked from their sweating pores. Multiple corpses of employees and unfortunate clients littered throughout the saloon in a messy bloody trail. The scene was morbidly disturbing. The mortality of it all held the brothers in an obsessive state of mind, as relatively thick blood seeped from necks of a few. Deep stab wounds perforated the torso and sternum in the others. Blood smeared the fancy decorative walls. He flung the blade of his Bowie knife, thus blotting the mirrors that surrounded the saloon's enclosure.

"This should make her itch," the brother declared while casually stepping over the straining woman who had her hands clasped to her neck, from the swipe of his knife across her throat. Nonetheless, the woman's blood gushed between her fingers, as her legs kicked about desperately. She began to gurgle helplessly, her eyes bulging with fear. "The nerve of that bitch!" he ranted. "She was real meticulous. We have always been three steps ahead of her." He wiped his bloody knife on the nylon garment that was worn by the woman who sat in the chair, her eyeballs hung barbarously from her skull.

He approached his brother, as he nonchalantly continued his speech. "It's as if somebody told her of our next move, and the only person that comes to mind is Julio." The man instantly became peeved.

"It wasn't Julio," the brother stated.

"And you sure about that?"

"What would Julio have to gain by selling us out?" the brother replied. "Come on, brother, I'm not too surprised if she just figured it out. We know her operation like the back of our hand. You do realize we are not dealing with a local type of chick here."

The brother listened but didn't like what he was hearing. He frowned. "But this is where we make Ms. Jessica McCray realize the worst thing in life is to make an enemy out of your friend." He chuckled.

"*Si, señor.*" His state was haggard, pessimistic even, as he was crazily fixated on a pool of blood beneath his footwear. Through his fascination, his voice whispered ghastly, "It's time to stop toying around. We going to lay low. Get her off edge, and when she least expect it, her brains is going to be in her lap." He pulled a cigar from the inside of his python skin suit jacket. He began chewing its stub, as the cigar protruded from the side of his mouth. The two brothers glanced at each other, sharing so much of the same characteristics that it was seemingly uncanny.

*****

Jessica paced for what appeared to be hours. Her behavior was persnickety. She was both emotionally and physically disturbed. Her arm was supported by a sling, sustaining minor injuries from that gunshot wound. Julio and two of her killers watched from a distance, while Jessica shouted obscenities into her cell phone. After she ended her boisterous phone conversation, Jessica dispelled the agonizing transmitter from her hand and tossed it over her shoulder disorderly.

"Look!" Jessica snatched the remote from the foot of her bed and muted *the Godfather Part II* that played softly from her plasma screen. "Sh—— is getting real hectic. Them Lopez brothers is somewhere out there lurking in the shadows, and then I just got word this f——ing Luca Gussalli made a move." She exhaled strenuously. "I don't understand how I am paying out all this money to killers like you." She approached one of the young gunners and nudged his head aggressively with the thrust of her figure. "I still have enemies." Jessica swiftly directed her evil eye toward Julio who posed a coolness

in his demeanor. "I got to play a ghost until we get all this b——
resolved. I'm purchasing a house in Ohio. Julio I still need you to
balance out shipments and oversee all the distribution. Everything
will remain the same. The only difference is my location." Jessica
sighed, as worry settled in her features.

Julio walked toward Jessica and graced her shoulder. "Yo, all
that ain't even necessary, Jess. You ain't got to go anywhere. We got
you. Just relax, yo. As you once said, the only thing that comes with
rushing is a crash course collision, yo. Just be patient," Julio said
decorously while easing her over to the side of the bed. "Now, get you
some rest, yo. Calm your thoughts."

Jessica obliged, as she lay herself in the comforts of her enormous
canopy bed. "You got a team of twelve men downstairs and another
six around the perimeter. No worries!" Julio's gesture of comfort
easily disarmed her cantankerous presentation. Instantly as Jessica's
head hit the pillow, she nearly collapsed into a state of lethargy.

"Without fear, we have nothing," Jessica spoke slow and
languorous.

*****

Detective Winsten was on his fourth bottle of cheap booze.
He was still sitting in his living room, staring overwhelmingly
at the lifeless young girl. It's been twenty-six hours since that
horrifying incident that completely shattered the detective's world.
The blood that formed around the girl's head now only appeared a
stain. Although she looked peaceful, her expression was enthralled,
settling, even within her colorless complexion and bluish lips. The
detective looked disheveled. He was consumed by cocaine mixed
with crushed prescription pills and was highly intoxicated. He
mumbled incoherently. His eyes were swollen; traces of tears ashed
the remorse that sustained his drooping features. His thoughts was
fuzzy, and his actions were unpredictable while carelessly fumbling
with the cylinder of his .44 Colt revolver. Sorrowfully he knelt beside
her, slowly stroking her hair and caressing her cold skin. He allowed
himself to explore the vacancy that was held in her glossy pupils. He

collapsed onto his back, facing the ceiling. His vision slowly started to diminish, as the room began to spin. His head felt heavy. He earnestly angled his arm, placing the shiny pistol firmly to his temple. The detective's hand trembled, while his finger fiddled with the trigger. A streaming tear spilled from the crevice of his iris. So many images flashed before his eyes so vividly, as he stared confusedly. Suddenly, a large man obscured his sight. The detective's eyelids lazily blinked, as he looked up miserably. The hooded villainous man stood above him in a threatening manner, placing his huge boot painfully on his wrist. The detective slightly grimaced, while he squirmed to free his hand. The pistol was awkwardly twisted in his grasp. The beast of a man looked down on the detective through demonic eyes, before the words trailed a chilling announcement.

"I'm here to inform you that your services are no longer needed." He delivered a precise cut in one sweeping stroke with the blade of his machete, mercilessly slashing the detective's throat. Blood spurted from his neck momentarily, before it simply commence to drain from his artery. The man removed his hood, bent down, and stared deep into the detective's terrified eyes, as he choked violently. The man gave the dying detective an egotistic wink, followed by a smirk, leaving that to be the last thing the detective saw, before darkness concluded his existence.

# CHAPTER 14

Three months later, ABL was released from Ross Correctional Institution (RCI). This is where he met Jessica McCray, on a dating Web site (pof.com), when he used to have a contraband cellphone. They hit it off instantly and eventually became long-distance lovers. They created such a bond through e-mails, letters, video, visits, and simply phone conversations. It was deemed to be unbelievable. ABL certainly had a way with words and at handling Jessica's heart, which ultimately captivated Jessica beyond her wildest dreams. It wasn't about having a man to fall in love with her for his own financial gain, but rather to love her for who she was.

ABL had five years remaining on his sentence once they actually evolved into one. There was just something about her. Besides her stunning looks and stupendous curves, he simply adored her mind. Jessica was indeed a smart young lady, but ABL didn't realize just how smart she really was. It's one thing to be smart and another to be sly. Technically, ABL didn't know Jessica as much as he assumed. All he understood was only what she wanted him to know. As far as ABL was concerned, Jessica was an aspiring model and actress. Only time would reveal the extent of a person's intentions. This was a moment Jessica was anticipating. Time was surely on her side, but with time, all things are not what they seem to be. Often the wait of something is why a lot of people live for the moment, because it's something you can embrace right then and there. The future doesn't always promise what you expect.

Despite Julio's convincing words, Jessica followed her intuition and bought a moderate-looking home in the suburbs of Bexley, Ohio. The neighborhood was a colony of lawyers, doctors, bankers, and investors, a small Jewish community that was inconspicuous in their livelihood, drawn away from the hustle and bustle of life and its endeavors, merely through their wealth, arrogance, and simple complacent expressions that allowed Jessica's strong and influential presence and personality to go unnoticed. With prosperity not only comes with those who think with you, but also it comes with principle, leadership, and greatness.

****

In the prison parking lot, there was a sufficient number of family, friends, and loved ones of all races and genders anticipating the arrival of the fortunate souls that overcame the turmoil of a world within a world. Suddenly, ABL observed the black and chrome Porsche SUV just as Jessica described, parked at a distance, with two stocky Dominican-looking men standing along the side of it. ABL cut his way through the crowd and made his way over to the two awaiting men, who both wore smug expressions. ABL greeted the guys with a casual head nod, right before one of the men courteously opened the rear door, as the other man advanced toward the driver's side. The entire ride was remotely silent, maybe even odd, as ABL noticed one small detail—the guy in the passenger seat paid close attention to him through the rearview mirror.

ABL really didn't read into it as being anything out of the ordinary. He was more than just invigorated to be on the other side of the fence. The streets of Columbus was a nightmare, a gangland, with murders, robberies, and rapes, a typical combination that could possibly be sustained anywhere in the world. And he was in the midst of it all. The lack of guidance and an eighth-grade education, not to mention the lack of love and the abandonment of his mother, caused ABL to revolt against authority and ultimately against himself. He deemed to have replenished his train of thought and simply vowed to gain knowledge and understanding throughout life. It's to be said, one's choice of words expresses the way one thinks. The way one thinks shapes one's reality.

After spending fifteen years in prison, it was a mentally delicate and sudden transition back into society. It was as if he was starting life completely from scratch. It's like learning how to walk all over again, which is something that could actually be discouraging, which could lead a lot of convicted felons back to what they have always resorted to customarily.

Upon arriving at their intended destination, all three men exited the vehicle, and one of the two men was seen concealing a pistol in his waistband as he took the lead. The other one followed behind ABL nearly at a distance, as his eyes cautiously weaved up and down the street. Approaching the door, ABL allowed his natural instincts to kick in. Scanning the scene, he observed everything in one swift motion. The landscape was perfectly manicured. The small pond with all the exotic fish and water fountain pouring down off the rocks were extra impressive, including the colossal glass double doors with gold iron gates. What ABL didn't expect to take notice of was the number of secret service replicas that roamed the house, with the cuff of their wrist held close to their lips, whispering discreetly. Again, he didn't put too much thought into it. Maybe she had a stalker, you know the whole Hollywood thing. He laughed to himself.

The door was unlocked, so he looked over his shoulder, sensing a need for clearance or something. But the men paid him no attention, so ABL entered on. Walking through the foyer, the house appeared like a museum. Antique artifacts meticulously decorated the brownstone walls. Slow-footed he proceeded around the corner, and there she was. He halted, simply struck by a sight of his stunning queen applying Palmer's Cocoa Butter to her thick thighs and legs and looking very appealing in her pink boy shorts and sexy Under Amour sports bra. She glanced up at him, instantly bearing a cheesy smile before bolting off the couch and into ABL's arms.

"Oh my god! Hi, babe." Jessica was overwhelmed, as tears of joy flooded her eyes. ABL clasped her tiny body firmly. Just the feel of her flesh and that certain scent of a woman were things he considered he missed the most. After a moment of their bodies being entangled like a twisted hanger, she leaned back just enough to kiss him on his desirous set of lips. "Damn, babe. Look at you handsome," she exclaimed while taking a step back to lustfully analyze every inch of him.

ABL unbashfully returned the gesture, as his beaming brown eyes burned a hole through Jessica's soul. Her hands slowly caressed his biceps, and her nipples came to a peek, as easily he stood aroused, a smile emerging on his glowing face. His dream seemed to be playing out right before him, as the woman of his imagination looked up at him, again with those beautiful peachy eyes. Tenderly he touched her cheek, furtively moving across her smooth skin with the back of his hand. Without any reluctance, she stepped toward him and felt the warmth of his breath, as his lips neared her neck, but he didn't kiss her just yet.

Gracing his touch to the spine of her back, he pulled her even closer, and she lightly moaned, as she appeared to have just collapsed in his embrace. Eagerly Jessica smoothly removed ABL's tight-fitting V-neck and passionately glided her hands across his striking physique while seductively enticing him with a lascivious stare. Instantaneously Jessica fondled with his thriving erection through his sweatpants. Her expression stated a sense of approval, as she slowly and gingerly pulled at his length, biting on her bottom lip. Then Jessica ardently freed his knotted drawstring from its restraint. She kissed him from under his chin, down his chest, to the peck of his amazing abs with the softest of kisses. The tender sensation had ABL a bit restive with every touch and display of her luscious lips. Anxiously she sat back down, perched up on the edge of the ostrich trim and leather love seat. Hastily she stripped him completely naked, assisted by a naughty spark steaming from her blooming caramel skin. A guileful grin formed on her face, her cheeks nervously blushing, before Jessica took hold of his hardened shaft and leisurely inserted his ponderous extremity into the warmth between her fleshly lips.

ABL was extremely vivacious seeing that Jessica went the whole extent, taking all of his long and thickness without a gag. Her eyes darted upward, and she knew indeed that he was loving every bit of it. Jessica deep-throated him one more time while maintaining eye contact, before popping her neck in rhythm. She went berserk on the dick, as if this has been the only thought on her mind. Back and forth, faster and faster she went, guiding with her hand to follow each motion of her lips. ABL tilted his head toward the ceiling, as his body rose off the tip of his Nike Air Precision NBKs. Jessica's mouth tactics were outrageous, and ABL saw the excitement she received from sucking his dick. The feeling was truly defined, yet slightly too much to withstand. He forced his urge to backpedal like all in his prime.

Jessica always seemed to find a way to get the best of a guy, as her appetite and addiction for a dick engulfed ABL. He gradually retrieved his allure from the profoundness of her salivating mouth, though a yearning Jessica wasn't so much compelled to. Gently but firmly, she gripped the foundation of his entirety, luring him back to the gaping of her mouth, where the gold ball of her tongue ring moved about teasingly. She began hitting him off with even more of the shrewdest head game, sloppy wet, as spit just trickled from the side of her mouth. ABL dug his fingertips into her scalp, feeling a rush of pleasure electrifying his body. His eyelids flickered, rolling his eyeballs to the back of his head, like a back-alley junkie.

After his warm cum oozed down her throat, Jessica pridefully acknowledged him with a big smile yet a little bashful, as she used the back of her hand to wipe the corners of her mouth. Jessica stood to her feet, his hands roaming wildly across her silky body, impatiently removing the fabric from her skin. He cuffed her buttocks in the palm of his grasp.

"I'm 'bout to have fun with this," ABL softly spoke, before he spun Jessica around, instantly becoming fascinated by her flawless backside.

Jessica bent over and parted her legs, eager to feel him, just as much as he was eager to feel her. He pushed inside her tight wetness, his knees becoming incredibly weak. He was astonished, as he thrust his massive member deep within her pussy, till he could go no farther. Jessica gasped, as ABL grabbed her tiny waist and began f——ing her with great endurance. He watched with a fatuous excitement, while Jessica's monstrous ass waved back and forth ferociously. ABL wasn't really a man of too many words, as Jessica's moans grew stronger and her vocalization escalated. He simply removed one hand from her waist and smacked her on the ass with a slight sting. She heaped forward, spotting a quick glance over her shoulder, marked with an expression of pain and pleasure. He twisted and grinded all inside her, filling the room with a clamorous sound. Jessica's defensive game was wearing thin, as it appeared she was fervent to climb over the back of the love seat. Vigorously Jessica's attempt was foiled by a mere tug of her waist. She sucked air between her teeth. His forearm rested sternly on the center of her back, as she pressed her body downward and lifted her ass farther in the air. After a few more thrust, ABL felt that urge again, and that tingling sensation was more intensive. His genitals tightened, and Jessica's big ol' ass played on his mind, as the vivid images of Black Chyna and Nicki Minaj intruded his imaginative sense. ABL pulled out, his dick reflecting a sparkling lustrous shine. Eagerly Jessica turned around and engulfed his member just as he released, once again discharging an abundance of thick semen in her mouth, spurting wildly and uncontainably.

# CHAPTER 15

"I know exactly where she is," Julio stated.

"Well, with you knowing where she is and us not knowing is not part of our agreement," one of the Lopez brothers spoke with a scowling look. He sat back nonchalantly. Nevertheless, Julio understood the severity of the situation, as he eyed the twenty-four-carat gold-plated snub-nose revolver, while his brother brandished a chrome and black riot pump. He walked in a stiff, haughty manner.

"Y'all been layin' so low in the cut. I haven't heard nothing from y'all since that last stash house thing," Julio said, slightly nervous, as he strained to keep his equanimity.

"Of course, you mean when Jessica coincidentally showed up as a f——ing UPS driver, killing two of my men, not to mention almost killing me and my brother."

"Yo, my apologies on that. She was real secretive. I don't know anything about it until after the fact," Julio replied confidently.

The brother with the pump held in his grasp looked skeptically at Julio. He really didn't like Julio, let alone trust him. He couldn't wait for his brother to give him that eye so he could blow Julio's head off his shoulders. He circled Julio, as if he was an animal being hunted for sport. Julio was feeling the intimidation, so he stood there with his hands remaining in his pockets. The sweat of fear trickled from under the brim of his New York fitted hat.

"So the question is, where is she?" the smirking brother inquired, as he whirled the revolver around his finger, like an old Western flick.

"She moved to Ohio, yo," he responded. "Some sh—— called Bexley. Yo, I got to go there a week from now to talk business," Julio further stated, before glimpsing over his shoulder. The man's presence behind him caused his skin to cringe. Julio knew he was at a disadvantage, despite the Glock 17 sitting next to the box of Apple Jacks cereal, directly in reach, temporarily enticing his murderous urge.

"Well, Julio." The man jolted to his feet, while his brother suddenly appeared at Julio's side, the riot pump resting harmlessly on his shoulder. He just stared at Julio while annoyingly sucking on his teeth. The residue of beef jerky reeked from his breath. "It looks as if we'll be taking a trip to Ohio," the man insisted. "That bowl of Apple Jacks looks good over there," he suggested with a slight nod of his head. "A killer like you, I'm so surprised you came to the door empty-handed." He chuckled. "I'm sorry your friend here wasn't as smart, yet a little braver, aye."

Julio's gaze shifted toward the floor. Julio clench his teeth. The body of Daz Juan Costello lay motionless with a chest full of buckshots and a Ruger .45 displaced at his side.

"It wasn't personal. Strangers and guns typically make my brother there a bit edgy," he insisted.

*****

"Bro, that nigga ABL been held captive by that bitch for like four days." Po choked before passing the blunt over to Decarlo. The herb smoke had Po's vision a bit hazy, driving down Republic Avenue, listening to Lil Wayne's *Carter V.*

"Yeah." Decarlo laughed. "Big bruh been playing that pussy like a tampon." He took a long drag, coughing almost instantly. He peculiarly looked at the greenish leaf that was pinched between his fingers. "Damn, cuz!" Decarlo patted his chest violently.

"I understood what Khari was saying about allowing nigga to get that fifteen years out of his nutz. Yeah, every nigga deserves that. But ABL ain't even coming out of the pussy to breathe." Coming up on Hudson Street, he made a left heading toward Cleveland Avenue. "We got business out here. Sh—— need to be discussed."

Po appeared to be agitated, as he declined the blunt from Decarlo's extended hand. Po was more than determined to have a face-to-face with ABL. Ever since Khari mentioned that New York hit him and ABL pulled off had Po feeling uneasy, just knowing the daughter of this once notorious man was now the queen of her throne and out seeking vengeance. He had nothing to go off besides the little information Khari gave him, but to make things even more unsettling, in the back of his mind, Po knew there was always somebody who knows somebody that knows about it.

"Hey, on another note, doe, did your sister text back?"

Decarlo quickly scrolled through his phone. Crossing Cleveland Avenue, Po came to a screeching halt, as the car in front of him slammed on its brakes at the red light on the corner of Joyce Avenue. Po reacted invidiously with obscenities. "Nah, bro. She didn't hit back yet," Decarlo replied. Po just shook his head. "You want me to try and call her real quick?"

"You shouldn't even have to. We talking about eight hundred thousand and no product. We producing fifty bricks a week, and she ain't responding." Po shrugged his shoulders, another explanation for Po's crudeness.

It was close to midnight, and he just left the bar, a bit tipsy off a few shots of tequila and six bottles of Bud Light. His phone was alerting of an incoming call. Assuming it was his baby mom, he ignored it. Just as much as he ignored everything else, he was caught up in his thoughts.

Neither he nor Decarlo who had his eyes glued to the activities on his phone paid any attention to the Lexus truck that pulled up right next to them. Po fumbled to light his cigarette. His eyes were slightly adjusted. He was certainly in a daze. The tinted window behind the passenger side of the Lexus slowly rolled down, a thirty-two-shot MAC-10 extended out the window and rapidly fired multiple projectiles, bringing forth a lustrous flash to illuminate the night, as shell casings littered the pavement. The first few bullets shattered the driver's side window, lodging into the dash and the headrest. Po quickly ducked in his seat and reached for his pistol. His reaction wasn't swift enough, as another barrage of bullets whistled through the night's air, hitting Decarlo in the head splattering his brain matter all over the upholstery. The bullets hit Po in his rib, hip, and thigh, and the one that pierced his rib bounced off a bone and traveled through his heart. Po helplessly fell from the car to the warm asphalt, and slowly he bled out, as the Lexus sped off around the corner. Again his phone alerted of an incoming call.

*****

"Now, niggas don't know how to answer the phone," Khari spoke to herself while sitting leisurely in some sexy attire in her luxurious Atlanta home that she shared with Daz Juan. Patiently she awaited his arrival. Khari indulged in a pint of cookies and cream while trying to focus on watching *American Horror Story*. Something just wasn't right. She had been calling Daz Juan nearly all day, and now Po wasn't answering his phone. Khari knew Daz Juan was going to Florida to handle some business. Jessica wasn't even on her mind, honestly. What was on her mind was the simple fact that Daz Juan mentioned something about Julio being there for Khari, which was a sure sign of trouble.

Julio was just one of those guys who stayed in the mix of things. He stayed plotting and living to get over on people. He had no loyalty, and the only thing he honored and respected was living by the sword. He would lie for no reason and simply make people believe he was someone that he wasn't.

With those thoughts swirling her mind, Khari attempted to call Daz Juan again, as she glanced out the window, hopeful that he would eventually be pulling up. Still there was no answer. Panic began to settle. She quickly texted her little brother before ringing Po's phone one more time, but the same results. *This wasn't like them*, she thought. She felt it. Something wasn't right.

# CHAPTER 16

Ten days later, after ABL was forced to bury his little brother and best friend, not even a week home, ABL was erratically rattled. He was devastated. Tormented, his heart weighed excessively. Despite his disastrous state of mind, ABL remained humble and assertive. He cruised the Columbus Street in his '86 Chevy Donk, the one Po got for him upon his release. Sadly ABL wasn't able to accept it from him personally. Its cotton-candy paint was fruity enough to blend with a glass of vodka. The clear coating reflected like a mirror. His chrome thirty-two-inch rims sat the car up like a truck, poking out from its chrome undercarriage like a fat lip. He was enjoying the mild weather while beating down the block with the aggressiveness of Dipsets and Hell Rell. ABL bobbed his head to the catchy lyrics while all the neighborhood spectators stared. Coming up North Sixth Street, ABL stalled momentarily, alluring a few big-booty hood chicks strolling by, puffing on a black and mild, trading faint giggles. ABL was amused and definitely intrigued. Nevertheless, he played it smooth. Jeopardizing his position with Jessica would be ludicrous. Jessica seemed to be blindly in love, and ABL took heed of that. On day one, she compensated him with a hundred thousand in cash and twenty-six outfits, twenty-six pairs of shoes, and twenty-six fitted hats, not to mention a brand-new black Jag, with the peanut-butter interior and black Lexani rims. Although ABL respected the muscle in old-school cars, the saying goes, "You can take a nigga out of the hood, but you can't take the hood out of a nigga."

Things were surely different to say the least. The world appeared the same, as far as one's expectation of life goes, but the people seemed more perplexed and complex. It was almost strange to be around humans, let alone interacting with them, as if he never existed. Just as things seemed weird to ABL, that was the same feeling with everyone else. For most, they thought or assumed he just came home from the army, simply from his militant ways and programmed mind-set. ABL even walked and had a certain type of difference about himself. One could tell there was something about him.

ABL yearned to be around people like him, but the streets seemed to have a curse on him, a wicked embrace that he just couldn't break free from. He roamed through what was considered to be the crime-ridden areas of the short north. He noticed the movement that was all too familiar, and it low-key thrilled him. No matter how much he read, studied, and self-disciplined his mental and physical states, ABL was who he was.

Nearing the liquor store on Fifth Avenue, he noticed a dark-skinned guy, with long dreads with blond tips hanging like a mane. He wore a tight-fitting shirt, fitted jeans, and some retro Grant Hill Fila shoes. He stood outside the liquor store profiling beside an orange Lamborghini Escalade, snacking on a bag of Fritos Honey BBQ. Two younger-looking cats, between the ages of sixteen and eighteen, were attentively standing guard at the rear of the vehicle. One of them was a few feet away, gingerly looking up and down the street, with his hands stuffed in his stonewashed jeans, chewing on a piece of gum.

ABL pulled into the parking lot, parking askew with all the other cars. He quickly caught the attention of everyone outside. Cockily, ABL hoped out of the car. His fitted polo jeans cuffed over his wheat Timberlands, he rocked a crispy polo button up and a Boston Celtic fitted hat, which coordinated with the color of the green stripes in his polo top and stitching in his dark-blue denims. His canary diamond-studded chain dangled to his midsection. ABL looked like a D boy or a walking lick, depending on how the man with the dreads chose to view his sudden approach. ABL understood the streets were nothing like they were fifteen years ago. He knew being out there was a risky move. This was a new generation, with a whole different set of rules. These new niggas didn't have any respect. It wasn't even about a name anymore. It was merely all about catching a body. ABL wasn't slipping. Concealed in his waistline was a semiauto 9 mm Luger. He walked past the mugging young cats, hitting them up with a simple head nod, and headed toward the dread, striding in pure confidence.

"What up, bro?" ABL greeted the man with his hand extended.

The man examined him suspiciously, before embracing ABL's hand into his with a firm clutch. "What up, doe?" the man replied. His eyes were red and slightly open. It was obvious that he was high. "Do we know each other or something?"

"Nah, but hey, my name is ABL." He introduced himself. Soon as he did, he could feel the heat from the young boys peering over his shoulder.

"Oh yeah, where you from, homeboy?" the guy asked with a grin, exposing a mouth full of crushed diamonds.

"I'm from Seventeenth and Cleveland," ABL answered with a shift in his stance.

The man eased closer, as he tossed back a handful of chips. "Bro, I never seen you before. And I damn sure ain't heard of you," the man claimed with hostility. The tension was building, but ABL wasn't about to fold. His demeanor was unrattled, and the look in his eyes was daring.

"I have been locked up for fifteen years, my nigga." ABL paused for a quick second, as the man appeared flabbergasted. "I been home for like two weeks, bro." The dread glanced over ABL's shoulder to his tricked-out Chevy and then toward his extravagant chain and costly apparel. "I'm just trying to get my hand in something and by the look of things"—ABL eyed the escalade—"you seem to be that guy to point me in the right direction."

"My nigga, you look straight," he said.

"Naw, not really. It just look good. I need a plug for me to be straight," ABL replied.

"A plug, huh?" The dread looked around nervously. "What you saying, bro? You the fed's playboy?" By now, the cats behind him were breathing down his neck, as the man in front of him approached even closer.

ABL knew he placed himself in a sticky situation. "C'mon, man. Hell naw! I ain't no f——ing feds. Ask somebody you know about me. The streets know me." ABL shifted his gaze while addressing all three guys. They all just gave ABL a grisly look.

"Okay, bro. What you trying to get into?" The man waved the boys off. "Please don't waste my time, dude. You seem like you 'bout that paper. You got my attention. What's up?" he popped another handful of chips in his mouth.

"I got eighty thousand I'm trying to spend. But, bro, I ain't trying to deal with a middle man."

ABL drifted within his thoughts. Khari just had Po and his little brother flipping bricks all through the city and millions in cash stashed somewhere with nobody knowing anything about it. ABL came home already the man without even having to break a sweat. He was set. Khari knocked off the infamous Daz Juan Costello and flooded the market with reduced prices that ultimately dominated the coke game. Khari stuck to the script, as she said she would. She held it down remarkably, though since the murders, Khari went astray. Now he was broke and back to square one, compelled to live off Jessica. To be out in the streets, risking it all, trying to catch his wave, he was simply a man, a convicted man with an ambitious state of mind.

"Bro, I'm not about to put my money in just anybody's hand, especially no eighty grand."

"If you are who you say you are and truly about your business, bro, I will introduce you to the right person for such a conversation," the man replied. He walked to the back of the SUV and popped open the latch from a remote device attached to his keyring. ABL followed his lead. "Let me show you something," the man said. He pushed another button, and the whole floor panel lifted, exposing a hidden compartment. Within its enclosure, perfectly compressed blocks were stuffed inside, wrapped in green duct tape. The smell was strong, reeking of pure kush. ABL nodded his head. "That's five hundred pounds of the highest-grade weed, straight from the border. If it's a plug you want, I gotcha," the man boasted.

"So what's up? Take my number and let's catch up," ABL eagerly suggested. The nine to five aspect wasn't sealing the deal. He felt as if something was missing. One thing for sure, he wasn't going to depend on Jessica's success for his means of living. ABL built his name off being what he only know he could be, a gangster.

"Naw, bro. Ain't no need for any phones. Just meet me back here tonight at nine, not 9:05, not 9:15. Nine o'clock, nigga. And I suggest you don't drive that car, doe. Be low-key as possible, and have your game face on, playboy," the man said.

Just then, a white-on-white 745 pulled into the parking lot, and behind the steering wheel was a highly attractive Asian-looking chick, listening to "Rhapsody." The dread swung open the passage door. "Don't disappoint me, cuz," he stated, before he hoped inside. The younger cats jumped into the escalade and pulled off, while the BMW slowly followed. ABL nodded impressively.

# CHAPTER 17

"Well, the evidence is very bleak. What you see is what you get." The FBI agent appeared frustrated, as he stood over the headless bodies discovered within a shallow grave.

"Four bodies, multiple gunshot wounds and beheaded. Has cartel written all over it," Agent Zelisko declared. "This is so ironic," he muddled. "It just might be in connection with our dead detective. This guy here"—he pointed to one of the contused bodies—"is surely tied in with the Lopez brothers." Agent Zelisko noticed the distinctive brand on his left arm. "Shell casings suggest they were shot after being dumped in this here grave." He walked meticulously with his head to the ground, analyzing the scene.

"Why would you imply that this is connected to Detective Winsten, sir?" the puzzled agent inquired.

"Because Detective Winsten was dirty as much as this ground beneath my feet." The agent looked at Zelisko appalled. "The man had a contract on his life, and it wasn't because he did his job impeccably as a homicide detective. This is Fort Walton Beach. There is not much going on here besides a bunch of young punks looking to get laid, high, or drunk. Of course, until you add the likes of mobsters and cartels, then we end up with crime scenes like this," agent Zelisko calmly explained.

"So your allegation is that the murder of Detective Winsten was a contract killing?"

"I think with the murder of Detective Winsten and the murder of these guys, someone is cleaning house," Agent Zelisko responded, before bending down and picking up a shell casing with the tip of his pen. He studied the imprint off the back of it, placed the casing inside a plastic bag, and handed it to a lab tech who was at his side snapping pictures. "I have a sensitive case building on a woman by the name of Jessica McCray. Does the name ruffle any feathers?" he questioned with a deep stare.

"Jessica McCray," the agent repeated, as he seemed to be in thought. "Of course, sir. Jessica McCray, the woman we had cased up in Chicago on cocaine distribution and conspiracy to commit murder. I believe the vic was her ex-boyfriend. Her father was the kingpin Fernando. Both he and her mother were brutally killed outside of a local ice cream shop in Manhattan," the agent recited, as if it was geographic quiz, which certainly gathered the respect of the more seasoned agent, who looked at him with such wonder.

"Impressive! Yes, that Jessica McCray. It appears that she has fallen right into her father's footsteps, with the help of the late Detective Winsten. He was said to have close connections with a few crime families, not to mention his close association with Jessica McCray. Investigation entails that a Mr. Antonio Demarco mistakenly killed Mr. Luca Gussalli's sons. The two bodies were meant to be the bodies of the Lopez brothers," Agent Zelisko spilled the script fluently, leaving the other agent astonish.

"Luca Gussalli. That's a big name," the agent acknowledged. "Antonio Demarco," he repeated. "That's a familiar name," he contemplated.

"What's even more familiar, once again, this was a man who was intimately involved with Jessica McCray. It could be a coincidence, but it's odd, the amount of bodies piling up next to this woman," Agent Zelisko said.

"So what's hindering her arrest?" the agent inquired.

"Arrest her on what?" Agent Zelisko chuckled. "We don't have anything substantial against her."

"What about the CI?" he encouraged.

"Ms. McCray seemed to be a bit crafty. She said less as possible, and she is never in the same room with the drugs and money. It's as if she kept avoiding every snare we set. So it's like we don't have anything to go off." Zelisko continuously scanned the large wooded area, as blood smeared a disturbing trail through the dirt. "This right here was a message intended for the Lopez crew."

"If Detective Winsten was so loyal to Ms. McCray and these bodies in this ditch are connected with the Lopez brothers, as you say, what makes this incident connected to the detective's murder?"

"Because often when people reach a certain position of superiority, those you once trusted have the tendency to be who you have to kill. It comes with sacrifices. Everyone is expendable. This is how these people think. So why wouldn't the detective's demise be connected to this?" Agent Zelisko looked at him sternly. "Sometimes you got to think outside of the credentials, Agent Pisaro."

"I never looked at it like that. Such an interesting concept. As the old saying goes, you got to think like a crook to catch a crook." A smile expressed his admirable features.

Zelisko motioned over a few other FBI agents, he pointed through the dense trees and whispered discreetly. Zelisko trained his attention back to Agent Pisaro, who was engaged in a sequence of rapid thumb movement upon the screen of his phone. Agent Pisaro looked up, only to lock eyes with a piqued Agent Zelisko. Quickly he put his phone up and adjusted his tie and neared Zelisko, as he cleared his throat. "So with all that summarized, if I'm not intruding, what do you have in mind to formulate a plan to actually apprehend Ms. McCray?" Agent Pisaro urged.

"First we must get something solid on her. If you remember correctly, the reason she was able to beat those federal charges is because of witness intimidation and the fact that the key witness was found hanging in some shabby hotel room just hours before testifying. She certainly knows what she is doing, and we obviously know what she is capable of," Agent Zelisko explained.

Agent Pisaro nodded in agreement. His face was that of a teenage boy. He had no facial hair, not even an inkling of stubs on his skin. His eyes were a deep blue with an enamored appeal to his stare. "In the meantime, we add this to the archive of all the other headless bodies discarded by the hands of the cartel. It's all considered to be just another question of, who did it? And why? A lot of tedious paperwork for the same thing that's bound to happen tomorrow. The more power a person achieves, the more violence they have to display."

*****

Sitting patiently in a rented Tesla outside of the Columbus Airport, waiting for Julio's flight to arrive, suddenly her phone vibrated in her hand. Keenly she swiped at her screen. The message simply read, "You got a mole within your organization." Jessica sighed deeply, as she clenched her phone. She considered carefully, as all the different names came to mind. Just then a soft tap sounded from the passenger window. Without even looking, Jessica unlocked the door from a button on her door panel. She set her playlist to Meek Mill's latest album *Championships* and *Oodles o' Noodles Babies* was transmitted from the car speakers in moderation.

"Yo, what up, Jess?" Julio spoke in a dry tone, as he and Jessica slapped palms.

"What's up with you? Why you sounding like that?" Jessica looked at Julio and noticed the pain in his face. She could tell something was disturbing him terribly.

"Hey, somebody killed Daz Juan, yo," Julio blurted out.

Jessica's complexion instantly lost its color, as it seemed the blood just drained from her face. She couldn't even speak. She was in utter disbelief. "Yo, he came to Florida, we talked over lunch, and we was 'pose to meet up that evening. But, yo, he never showed up. I kept calling his phone, but he never answered, yo. So. I went to the hotel he was staying at and found him shot in his room, dead, yo!" Julio passionately lied.

"Julio, what the f—— did you do?" Her brows contracted into a frown.

"Yo, I didn't do nothing. Word is bond. I'm telling you what happened. Somebody killed him, yo," Julio said.

Jessica rolled his eyes. "And the money?" She looked out her window toward the parked cards. What she didn't take into account was the Dodge Ram 1500 sitting three cars behind her, which was occupied by the Lopez brothers. They landed in Columbus two hours before Julio. The two men sat quietly with a .380 pistol equipped with a silencer resting on both of their laps, and an AR-10 with armor-piercing bullets laid upon the back seat. Their stare was empty. They were eager, but the airport was too risky. They had enough sense to rationalize. Besides, they knew Jessica never traveled alone, and they were right. Somewhere within the cluster of automobiles was a Chevy Impala, with four heavily armed shooters inside, watching Jessica's every move, not to mention the movement of others.

"I don't know about any money. Yo, we didn't get to that point. That's why we were 'pose to meet up that evening. Word, yo. We conversed over lunch. Everything was fine. You get what I'm saying? He said he was a little tired. I'm like, 'Bet, get you some rest and meet me at such and such at this time,' and that was that," Julio defended.

Jessica looked at him with the most hate. She knew Julio wasn't telling the truth, and for him to lie to her, she knew there was more to it. Nevertheless, she had to contain her emotions. "Julio, when you got to the room, what did you do?" Jessica asked, going against her urge to retrieve her .40 from under the seat.

"I knocked on the door a few times. Then as I'm looking around waiting for him to answer the door, yo, I sees the rental, so I know he there. I started banging on the door, yo. Still nobody answered. I tried to open it. It was locked. So I went to the front desk and offered shorty a hundred bucks to key the door, and yo, there he was, B."

"So you didn't go in? Didn't make any attempt to look for the money? Maybe get the car key and rummage through the vehicle, huh? Nothing like that?"

"Yo, you know I'm a convicted felon. I'm not even supposed to be outside the state of New York. I wasn't about to contaminate the scene with my DNA. I told shorty to call the cops, and I got up out of there." Julio fabulously fabricated his story, as he sat there convinced.

"Oh, the cops, huh? So that means a newspaper article and news coverage, public spectators, and everything, right?" Jessica insisted.

"C'mon, Jess. Yo, we better than that. I didn't come all the way up here just to lie to you," Julio replied. "You left me in charge of the business. I'm here to handle business, not sabotage it."

Jessica gave him a doubtful glance.

# CHAPTER 18

"Listen, I understand we may have gotten off on the wrong foot," Fernando spoke with his usual whisperlike tone, as he partook of a casual glass of Hennessy on the rocks. "I would like to put all that frivolous sh—— behind us. I need to ask something of you, something that I can't bring to nobody else."

"Fernando, all that ain't even necessary, my friend. We share a mutual respect for each other. It's always business, never personal," Devecchio said through a raspy voice. He nursed a glass of whiskey in one hand and puffed on a cigar with his other hand. "So what brings you to Little Italy?"

"Well, actually, there really isn't any other way to say it, but my wife is having an affair," Fernando said. A sense of embarrassment sounded in his tone. He took a big gulp of his drink.

Devecchio was taken aback. "Are you about to try and proposition me to kill your wife?" He looked at Fernando seriously. "Despite my profession, women and children I don't do."

"No no no." Fernando chuckled. "Not at all. That's not why I'm here. It's probably even more complicated than that."

Devecchio stared at him full of perplexity. Fernando dug into his pocket and pulled out the extravagant-looking necklace, a folded piece of cloth, and a skeleton key. He placed the items in front of Devecchio, as they both leisurely stalled at the bar. Devecchio glanced at the eccentric-looking things, before looking back to Fernando, with the anticipation of an explanation.

"It might be far-fetched, but I have a gut feeling that my wife's affair might get me killed one day." Fernando's eyes trailed off. He thought deeply, swirling the ice cubes within his glass. He was reluctant to speak. He mused over the idea of the man he trusted to ultimately betray him to the point of wanting everything Fernando strived for, including even his family.

"Fernando, that's a strong assumption. Why would you even consider that to be an option? That sounds semiridiculous," Devecchio said.

"It's only ridiculous if you choose to view it as being something funny," Fernando replied. "And to answer your question, it is because certain things play on your mind for a reason. I'm just following my intuition. I'm feeling the change in my wife and in my closest associate, with whom she is having an affair with. If love is lost and the trust is betrayed, you have nothing. There's just two people formed against you, one who wants to get rid of you and the other who wants to replace you." Fernando took another swig of his Hennessy, before Devecchio reached under the bar and grabbed another bottle of Hennessy and refilled his glass graciously.

"Damn! That's a hard pill to swallow," Devecchio admitted. "And what about these?" He made reference to the items situated on the counter.

"I have a daughter. Her name is Jessica McCray. If something were to happen to me, I need her to get these things so that she'll know the truth," Fernando spoke with a sorrow-stricken utterance.

"So basically you just want me to get in touch with your daughter and simply give her this stuff?" Fernando assured him with a nod of his head. Devecchio picked up the necklace, slightly mesmerized by its sparkling jewels. "This is such an extraordinary piece."

"It's been passed down from generation to generation. It was last worn by Pablo Escobar's ex-wife, before it graced the neck of my wife," Fernando explained.

"It must have one hell of a curse on it." Devecchio laughed. Fernando stealthily released a smirk, but quickly dismissed the poor sense of humor from his expression. "Excuse me, Fernando." He reached over and grabbed Fernando's shoulder in a manly fashion. "I didn't mean nothing by it. Just trying to lighten up the situation."

Again Fernando nodded his head, before Devecchio held up his glass. Fernando followed suit, and their glasses clicked in a friendly toast. "I'll be honored to do that for you. An unusual request, but it's doable."

\*\*\*\*\*

Khari roamed the Linden Area, the north side of Columbus. Her clothes were extremely filthy. She lost an undetermined amount of weight. Her skin was blotched. Her hair was shabby-looking. Her body ached and shivered from her urgency to get high. The murder of Daz Juan, Po, and her brother Decarlo caused Khari to give into a needle and a bag of heroin for her emotional support. She was lost within herself. Every step she took was another drastic measure. She even resorted to selling her body to all the local drug boys and knuckleheads. She was so disreputable she couldn't muster up enough doughtiness to face ABL. Khari was full of ignominy. She was broken. All she could think of was getting her next fix, she needed to feed her veins, but she was struggling. All she had was $1.75 in her pocket. Walking down Loretta Avenue, Khari spotted Ja emerging from a known drug house.

"What's up, Ja?" Khari shouted at a distance, as she hastened her step.

Ja looked at her outrageously. "Girl, you know better than to be blasting my name like that." Ja chirped the alarm off his two-toned, rimmed-up Cutlass Supreme. "What you want?" he asked with an attitude.

"Ja babe, don't be like that." She moved jerkily. Ja walked right past her, paying her no attention, while she attempted to flirt. "Be a sweetheart, and let a girl hold a lil' something."

"K, c'mon now. You know it ain't no hand-to-hand sh——— outside the house. Go knock on the door. Bro and 'em up in there," Ja insisted impetuously.

"I don't have any money, Ja," Khari whined. "That's why I'm approaching you. Besides, them niggas be acting too cocky."

"So what do you expect me to do?" Ja questioned, as he hung over the roof of the car. Khari's shoulder shrunk, while she shyly looked toward the ground.

"I was thinking." She hesitated. "Maybe I can give you some head or ass for a fix." She sniffled the mucus running from her nose. Ja looked her up and down, considering the offer, for he always had a thing for Khari. Ja was one of Decarlo's closest friends. It was excruciating to see Khari in such a state of distress, but Ja couldn't allow himself to get caught up over something he sees every day. So he obliged.

"Yeah, whatever. Get your ass in the back seat. My baby moms will kick my teeth down my f——ing throat if she sees you in my sh——," Ja announced, as he settled in his seat. Briefly he scanned through the contents of his phone. "What's up? Where you want to do this at?" Ja smiled sheepishly.

"We can do it right here," Khari replied. Suddenly, Ja's head was snatched back, and the feel of sharp steel was firmly pressed to his quavering Adam's apple. Khari slowly licked the side of his face, before swiping the blade across his throat. She instantly leaned over and quickly rummaged through his pockets, as his neck began to hemorrhage. Khari removed a large roll of currency and a quarter bag of Mexican tar, along with a few baggies of crystal meth. Khari was ecstatic, as she eagerly got out of the car and simply cleared the scene.

# CHAPTER 19

ABL was peaceful yet felt a sense of guilt, as he relaxed in his boxers, shirtless and sweaty, while watching the evening news. Cum saturated his thighs and genitals. His mind was settled, and he was pretty much at ease, while he eyed the neatly stack of cocaine bricks next to his bedside. Successfully his plan went through without any strife. He was hesitant and extremely leery at first. ABL simply just smiled. Suddenly, the sound of the shower became mute, as a motionless moment passed before she entered the room. ABL ogled. Her body glistened from the pebbles of water sprawled across her soft and seemingly warm flesh. Playfully she hopped on ABL and added a slew of kisses to his neck and face. He gripped her ass firmly, and his hormones certainly got the dance, as his nature again started to peak.

"Dude, you were awesome. I never knew delivering drugs reaped the benefit of some good dick." She giggled. "Where did you learn how to f—— like that?" she asked joyfully. A delighted smile emerged. Her Barbie dollish green, hazel eyes were just a daze. Her wet blonde hair dripped on ABL's chest, before she tossed her long stringy hair over her shoulder. ABL snickered.

"I know, right? I just love f——ing, I suppose." He appreciated the freckles on her face. "Or I just love f——ing white girls with a phat ass." They both smiled lustfully. ABL smacked her ass, his grip of it tightened, which brought forth an isolated moan. The excitement read all within her expression. She felt so comfortable with ABL. The feeling was a yearning desire, as if she been here before, attached to something so familiar, it was haunting.

"I'm so glad everything happens for a reason. Damn, you are such a hottie. I can't believe I'm this attracted to you right now." She stood up from his lap of sexual arousal and slipped back into her thongs and squirmed her T-shirt over her voluptuous breast. She maintained an enchanting switch to her hips while sashaying toward the bundles of coke. An eighth of a brick was busted down, divided into individual lines. She leaned forward, placing her face to the miniature table stand, inserted a rolled-up $100 bill into her left nostril, and deeply inhaled the scaly substance that slightly burned her inner passage and slowly streamed down the back of her throat. She instantly made an awful look but then smiled with a sense of exhilaration.

"That's some good sh——." She repeatedly sniffed. "Wow!" She spun around, flaunting her shapely figure. "How do I look?" she teased.

"Amazing," ABL replied. "Hey, when did you say you were leaving?" he asked, completely tantalized by her bowlegged stance and wide hips. "Naw, not like that." ABL smiled. "I'm saying far as going back to Florida," he added.

"Tomorrow morning. My flight is at ten. But I was actually thinking—" She paused. She looked at ABL full of uncertainty.

"Finish what you were about to say. You were actually thinking what?"

"You know, possibly kicking it with you a lil' more, show me around, and simply let me see how you living," she continued.

"Let's just end this night on a good note, and we'll see what the morning has," ABL responded. He grinned as she smacked her lips.

"Yeah, whatever. Boy, you ain't trying to get to know me. You probably don't even remember my name." She rolled her eyes.

"Caroline, a.k.a. Sapphire. Which name would you rather be called?" ABL quickly shot back, which caused her to express a sense of gratitude.

"I prefer Caroline. I like how that sounds. What about you?" She smiled, before finding her spot back on the bed next to ABL. Her touch brushed lightly up his thigh. "You must be used to cats smashing and disappearing, huh?" ABL rested up on his elbows just staring at her. Actually there was something intriguing about her.

"C'mon dude. I'm a stripper." She laughed. "I know how the game goes. Guys ain't trying to do nothing but smash. As you said,

I'm a white girl with a phat ass. My position in life is more lucrative face down, ass up." Her tone diminished slightly. Caroline stared off at a blank space on the wall. ABL could tell that she was in serious thought.

"Man, stop it!" He chuckled. "That stripper sh—— don't mean nothing. Either you going to hold it down with a nigga or you ain't. That's what guys look for in a woman. It's all about your strive and will. Real talk! If you can't see nothing in yourself, how you expect a nigga to respect you?" ABL confirmed.

"Awwww." She blushed. "Oh my f——ing god. I can't believe you just said all that." She stared at him for a moment, seeming absolutely surprised. "That's what's up. Thanks." She commenced to caress his chest. "You just don't strike me as being a street dude. You like a sweetheart for real."

ABL displayed a coyness about himself. "I mean, everyone has a past, and often your past can play into your future. It be the things in life that help you get to where you want to be, and that is the most complicated to shake," he replied.

"I just love listening to you," she admitted. "So what you got in mind right now?" Caroline asked modestly.

"I'm slipping. I got to get these bricks away from me and out of this room. I be back. Let me make this call real quick." ABL grabbed his phone off the edge of the bed and attempted to put his pants on.

"Hey, wait. Hold up." She stood in front of him, blocking his progression. "Who you about to call?" He tone was rushed. ABL looked at her peculiarly. She appeared overly anxious.

"Calm down," he suggested. "I'm about to call my guy. What's up?"

"I'm sorry." Caroline laughed nervously. "I was going to say you know in my line of work. I meet a lot of different people. So I was kind of figuring, let me work the package and earn points on it," she eagerly suggested.

ABL fell out laughing. "Look at you." He continued to express his hysteria. "What you know about points on the pack?"

"I'm not your average white girl." Caroline radiated a smile. "You see how I just hit the door with your delivery like Pizza Hut."

The two entertained a pleasant laughter. "I know people, see what I'm saying?" she urged.

"So, hey, you should be good with those people you know. This ain't that," ABL replied, dropping his smile, as he pushed past her while getting dressed.

"But I want to make money and have fun while I'm doing it," she asserted. Approaching ABL from behind, she wrapped her arms around his waist and gave soft kisses along his spine, while her hand fondled at his crotch. ABL's sexual drive was raging within his being. His thoughts prevailed to the visual of her ass energetically plunging against his pelvis.

*****

Outside in the parking lot of a motel somewhere on I-61, within the city limits of Columbus, awaited a group of gunmen inconspicuously lingering between vehicles, seeking their opportunity. Jessica was positioned a few feet away, discreetly behind tinted glass, inside a 2012 Camaro. She was reclined in the passenger seat, bumping Young MA's *Car Confessions* in the company of one of her lieutenants.

"I can't believe this f——ing ABL," Jessica declared, as she clashed her small fist into her open palm. "There's a lot of things we think a person won't do, but often it's the things that we don't consider that they will do." Her eyes were trained on the rearview mirror. Her heart beat anxiously. "Where the f—— is this bitch?" Jessica shouted, before checking her platinum diamond-studded watch.

"What about Julio?" he curiously inquired.

"I got that clown. Don't even trip," she replied.

*****

Back inside the motel, ABL finished conducting a few plays off his phone. The mood became odd. Caroline was now fully dressed, as was ABL, but he had his T-shirt draped over his shoulders. She sat silently on the bedside, while ABL finished up a few text messages. His demeanor was real standoffish, and Caroline was confused.

"ABL, I be back. I'm about to make a run to McDonald's. I'm starving. You want something to eat or no?" She stood up retrieving her car keys, hand purse, and cellphone nearby.

"That's cool. Hey, get me whatever you get," ABL replied.

She simply turned toward the door and extended her hand to open it. That was just a thought she had to put into someone else. She lazily opened the door, walked out, and slowly closed it behind her, without another look in ABL's direction. He noticed it, but assumed she was mad because he knew she wanted to have sex again. He laughed to himself, before stashing the bricks in a duffel bag.

*****

Caroline appeared in plain view, bypassing the assemblage of shooters scattered around, eyeing the parking lot looking for Jessica. Caroline's phone abruptly vibrated. She swiped the screen. "Look for the brake lights," her text message read. As soon as Caroline lifter her face from the glowing screen, she noticed the red lights illuminating from across the lot. Caroline moved toward the car, cautiously approaching the passenger side. The dark tint slowly rolled down, unveiling Jessica's alluring features, though her expression wasn't so appealing. Jessica was pissed.

"Damn, bitch! What were you in there doing?" Jessica spat angrily.

"I was doing exactly what I was paid to do," Caroline responded. "I had to play my role. Dude ain't stupid."

Jessica became slightly skeptical, as Caroline's energy perceived something else. "Anyway, if anything took place in that room other than what was instructed, I will personally put a bullet between your eyes." Jessica handed Caroline an envelope full of cash. "So what's up?"

"He really didn't say much about anything referring to Julio or anybody else. He basically just sent out a bunch of texts." Caroline spoke with a soft tone.

"For two hours? That's all you can tell me?" Jessica was fuming. "That sh—— don't even make sense. You ain't telling me nothing."

"Like I said, he ain't stupid. You want me to go back inside? He's expecting me to come back anyway," Caroline said with a malicious intent.

Jessica glanced at her smirking lieutenant, who simply shifted his gaze opposite of hers. "Expecting you to come back," Jessica repeated sardonically. "Why would you be coming back?" she asked through squinted eyes.

"I told him I was going to McDonald's real quick," Caroline explained.

"Naw, you played your role good enough. Go ahead and get ready to take your ass back to Jacksonville. I'll be in touch if I need to be," Jessica assured.

Before she walked back behind the tint, Caroline walked off with a mischievous smile. Once she was seen driving a Ford Focus off the pavement of the parking lot, Jessica spoke. "I can't believe that lil' bitch. Was she f——ing serious?"

Her lieutenant simply just shrugged his shoulders. "You think they f——ed?" Jessica asked desperately.

"What's our move now?" He ignored her frivolous thought.

"We just wait. Tell everyone to fall back?" Jessica instructed.

# CHAPTER 20

ABL quickly hopped in the passenger seat of that same BMW 745 he saw that day in front of the liquor store. He tossed the duffel bag in the back seat.

"Hey, good look, shorty. Here you go." He handed her a knot of cash. At first, she was in disbelief and really didn't know how to take to his overbearing show of generosity. Nonetheless, she accepted the roll of bills and stuffed it inside her Victoria's Secret.

"Thanks." She smiled. "Um, so now what?" she asked.

"Drop me off near Westerville Road. Just drive. I'll show you. But, hey, just drive easy, doe, yah hear me? No extra sh———. Just normal," ABL spoke firmly, without even peeking up from the screen of his phone. The woman gladly obliged, as she commenced to pull out from her parking space. Her curiosity of the man to the left of her caused her to sneak yet another glance in his direction. He still didn't take notice of her. She adjusted in her seat, as the bundle of money rested uncomfortably against her region. Also she observed the butt of his pistol sticking out from under his shirt. She was becoming not only nervous but also a bit excited.

"Excuse me." She turned the volume down on her phone, muffling the raspy sound of Jadakiss rapping through the factory speakers. "What did you say your name was again?"

ABL looked at her. His eccentric demeanor was reserved and calculated. His temperament was chilled, though his energy was very gloomy and reluctant. His mystic eyes appeared to pierce right through the young woman, while she awaited a reply. Forcing herself to appease him, she displayed a set of dimples.

"I never gave you a name," ABL said.

"My point exactly." She giggled.

"I'm just f——ing with you." He smiled. "My name is ABL, but you can call me Hush."

"Hush, huh?" She paused. "That's a good fit for you."

"Why you say that?"

"Because you don't seem like the talkative type. And honestly you just seem sneaky as f——," she joked. "I think I like ABL better." She flirted with an endless smile.

"I get a lot of that. Hey, you see that red Ford Focus over there?" He pointed toward a gas station on the right-hand side of Cleveland Avenue. "Pull up there," ABL directed.

She eased beside the car. Caroline looked over and was enthused once she saw ABL. She was completely unmindful of the pretty Asian chick sitting seductively behind the wheel. "Hold up real quick." He gathered his duffel bag and walked it over to the Ford. Caroline already had the trunk accessible. After securing the bag, ABL casually walked over to the driver side of the BMW. Bearing a brooding amusement, ABL rested his elbows on the frame of the window, but he didn't say anything. He just stared at the woman, a bit ridiculously.

"What?" she sheepishly inquired. "Why you looking at me like that? Ain't that your girl over there?" She presented a firmness, as she leaned away from him.

"If that was my girl, I wouldn't be over here all up in your face," ABL insisted. "I'm saying, doe, you know my name, but I didn't get yours."

"Maybe because I asked, and you didn't." Her sarcasm was evident. The chase she initiated was very much adoring. ABL was more than reacting on timing, not so much on impulse.

"Okay, Ms. Lady. This is me asking, what's your name?" He was smiling, but his tone was rushing.

"Yazmine," she simply responded, slightly at a whisper.

"Yazmine, listen, I appreciate you tonight, fo' sure. But if you trying to make some more money, you got my number. Catch up with me." ABL politely extended his hand.

"I got you." Yazmine softly took his hand into hers with a devilish gleam in her eyes, a gleam that would have tempted any man.

ABL stalled momentarily, before he regained his senses and retracted his hand. He earnestly walked away with a close examination of his surroundings. Once inside the Ford Focus, he let out a calm breath of air, and his head relaxed on the headrest. ABL coordinated his thoughts, still fully aware of the contraband that was being hauled just steps within his possession.

"We good?" Caroline took note of his disposition.

"Yeah, she with it," he mumbled. His phone sounded. He picked it up off his lap. It was a text from Jessica. He shook his head.

"What's wrong?"

"Naw, it ain't sh———. Make a left at the next street. When you get to the end of the street, turn right," ABL casually informed, before opening his text. "Babe, where are you? It's getting late. I'm starting to worry," it read. ABL sighed.

*****

Luca Gussalli was indecisive, as he stood behind the twelve-inch blade of one of Jessica's accountants. The knife pressed urgently to the man's perspiring throat, while Luca cowardly knelt before him.

"Where the f—— is she?" Gussalli yelled insanely.

"I don't know who you are talking about. I have multiple females that I associate myself with," the man whimpered.

"So you don't know who it is that you work for?" A wicked laughter echoed within the garage. "What's so funny, Mr. Bonilla, is I know exactly who it is that you work for. Isn't that so f——ing ironic?" Gussalli pressed the teeth of the blade harder against the man's flesh, slightly breaking the skin. A trickle of blood slowly eased unto the shiny, sharp surface and down his chest. The man's eyes were afflicted with terror.

"Pleeeeassse!" the man invoked pitifully. "I don't know what you are talking about." A stream of tears slid from beneath his eyeglasses.

"It appears everyone seems to have the same senseless answer when asked the question about this woman." He laughed. "I must admit I admire the devotion you have displayed. Sadly, the last guy I had in a similar situation as yours cost him the life of someone very important, I suppose. There is one option I'm willing to leave open, and that's allowing you to get up and walk out that door," Gussalli whispered, removing the knife away from the man's throat.

Luca Gussalli walked around the man and forcefully stood him to his feet. They were eye to eye, though Bonilla diverted his stare from Gussalli. "No, my friend look at me." Luca grabbed the man's chin, briskly turning his face back to where their eyes met once again. "You have no reason to be scared of me. You have probably seen just as much as I have, just from a different perspective, am I right?"

"Y…e…s," he stuttered.

"The only difference in what I see in your eyes is the hurt of having to live with the knowledge of not knowing what happened to your sons. In your heart, you have accepted the fact that they will never return. The only thing you got to go off is the name Jessica McCray." Gussalli studied Bonilla's nervousness at the mention of her name. "You can't even begin to imagine the pain of a lost child, let alone two of them." His speech halted. "This whole situation is more strenuous than you may allow yourself to rationalize."

"I don't have the information you want," Bonilla spoke timidly. Abruptly, two more men entered the garage. Catching Gussalli's eyes, they simply gave him a head nod and fell into place with the other guys who watched in sheer suspense. "I can ask around and see what I can find out," Bonilla added convincingly.

"Are you sure about that? You are hired to control and manage millions of dollars for this woman. Of all the people in the world, you don't know where she is? Or how to get in touch with her?"

"I have always received orders from a man by the name of Kevin Winsten. I don't know anybody with the name Jessica McCray. You can check all my statements and my bank receipt and deposits." Bonilla found his voice of certainty.

"Of course." Gussalli snickered. "Detective Winsten, right?" Bonilla nodded in agreement. "You do realize this Kevin Winsten you are referring to was murdered?" Bonilla appeared befuddled. "Sure you do." Gussalli glared. "You're right, my friend. No harm done."

He gently smacked Bonilla on his cheek and confidently departed with a perilous smirk. Once the last guy of the group disappeared, Bonilla happily balanced himself upon his wobbly knees. Exhaling heavily, he couldn't believe Luca Gussalli separate. In situations like this, at the mere thought of family, Bonilla raced out the garage. He approached the opened door that was located on the side of the house. Instantly a strange feeling occurred upon entry. Once he walked into the living room, he was faced with a horrific scene. The room was in total disarray. Blood was smeared throughout the room like a flinging paintbrush. Briefly he studied the area in disbelief. It was as if he was watching a movie, waiting for the next scene. His feet were planted like roots, as his eyes fearfully inspected every piece of broken glass to the ripped article of *Future* and clothing sprawled about aimlessly. Fixing his astounded stare at a broken picture frame of him, his son, and his beloved wife, he rushed to the bedroom, but all that played on his distraught mind was the well-being of his three-year-old son. Coming to a halt at his son's room, his eyelids suddenly were overwhelmed with tears. The carpet beneath him was soaked in bodily fluids. Bonilla seemed like a puzzle, shattered in a million pieces, pieces that reflected of a hopeless man.

Quickly sensing that he lost the one thing in life that truly defined him, a gut-wrenching explosion submerged within his stomach. It was evident his soul was drained from his being. With no more hesitation, he kicked the door off the things. There she was, the mother of his son, bound and gagged while hanging upside down in the middle of the room. Her naked and bruised body bore a large slash from her vagina to her throat, cut with precision. Blood slowly dripped from her body, forming a pool underneath. He glanced into the empty stare of the woman he loved so much. That's when he noticed his son lying in the bloody pool, with a single gunshot to his head. His innocent eyes gleamed into a fix daze, as Bonilla examined the boy's features who seemed to look just like him. He instantly collapsed to his knees, scooping the boy's limp body into his arms.

A yell of despair escaped from the silence. Pupils that pierced endlessly peered onward into a thin glassy coating of darkness, trapped in the mind frame of uncertainty. Bonilla's head just dropped, smothering his face into his son's belly. His speech was muffled, as he rocked back and forth, as if it was an ordinary night of rocking his son to sleep. His wet body was pressed against his father's. The red fluid stained his skin. The reality of it all was misleading to a sense, as each teardrop told a story, until falling into a puddle of nothing but a memory. Bonilla reluctantly released his son from his embrace, gently placing him on the floor and closing his eyelids, concealing his lifeless daze. In turn, he did the same with his wife, before granting her a kiss on her clammy cheek.

# CHAPTER 21

"Babe, you hungry?" Jessica yelled upstairs to ABL, just as he got up from the floor off his last set of push-ups. He admired his bulky physique in the full-length mirror. He smiled before racing down the stairs. Entering the kitchen, he spotted Jessica from behind. Her tiny shorts amazingly hugged her hips and thighs. ABL approached her with a tight embrace and a small kiss on her neck. Despite his sweaty body, she felt good being smothered in his biceps and the stiffness of his dick pressed firmly in the small of her back. She rotated her hips a bit teasingly. He laughed.

"Naw, what's up, doe?" He eased up. "What was you yelling?"

Jessica quickly turned around and lustfully looked him up and down. She just shook her head out of pure delight. *Damn!* was the thought she had in mind, but rather she just repeated what she had initially said. "I asked if you were hungry," she replied while attempting to preserve her focus. Her eyes nonetheless fell down to the bulge prolongated inside his Nike mesh shorts. *Oh my god!* was yet another thought that simply entered her mind.

"Yeah, that sounds perfect." ABL smacked his alluring abs. "A couple of grilled bologna and cheese sandwiches with some BBQ chips make sense to me," he said.

Jessica laughed heavily to the point she was bent over bracing herself off her knees. "Bologna and cheese sandwiches," Jessica mocked. ABL just looked at her while sipping on a bottled water. "Just go take a shower, and I'll have something down here waiting for you," she said with a zealous smile. Shifting her thick hips around the kitchen, Jessica reached over ABL, as he stood there in deep admiration. Her perky breasts brushed against him. Her long hair tickled his skin.

"I know that's right," ABL insisted.

She looked at him puzzled. "You know that's right, what?" Jessica asked. She was surprised, as she giggled slightly.

"I see you want to play, huh?" He discarded the half-empty bottle of water. ABL walked up on her again.

Jessica looked up at him with a yearning spark held in her eye. Her hand rested on his hard chest, as if she was trying to prevent his advance. Actually she started to caress every inch of him, before pulling him closer by a mere tug of his waistband. ABL leaned toward her and kissed Jessica on her soft and green-apple-flavored lips. He inserted his tongue just a little, and their lips were briefly interlocked. His hands eased down her spine, and then his fingers graced the split between her ponderous cheeks. Jessica managed a light sound of pleasure, right as he sternly palmed the cuff of her ass and lifted her onto the countertop, knocking the bowl of bananas, grapes, and apples to the highly polished wood grain floor.

Aggressively he pulled at her clothing until she was completely unraveled. Jessica fought against his urge as long as she could, simply for the excitement of it, but before she knew it, he was deep inside her, thrusting rapidly. Jessica's arms were locked around ABL's neck, and she appeared to be hanging on with all her might, while her moans filled the space with such blissful emotional sound.

ABL was digging in that pussy, as Jessica tenderly sank her teeth in his neck, tasting his salty flesh and inhaling the essence of his raging testosterone. She was overwhelmed by his force and so turned on by the forward movement of his pelvis that her juices committed to stream down her lovely thighs. Impressively ABL moved her from the counter to the nearest wall, her back plastered against it as a sheet of wallpaper. He continually worked her throbbing pussy like a man who knew the true anatomy of women. Her legs were securely wrapped around his waist.

ABL's strength was evident. He pushed up and down off the tip of his toes, bouncing her small frame up against the wall with every forceful push and urge. Jessica's body was tingling sensually. Her mind intervened with so many different thoughts of this man. Just his energy to deliver such a f—— had her so amazed. Her nails dug into his back, leaving long traces of marks from the middle of ABL's back to his massive shoulder blades. He grimaced, but the pain only seemed to power him up even more. Jessica abruptly felt herself being carried in the air, as if she was floating. Once she adjusted her eyes, she found herself awkwardly seeing things in quick sequences. Everything appeared to be upside down, and her body was twisted in midair before being slammed to the couch. "Oh sh———," she uttered. ABL threw himself on her, just as quickly as her body met the cushions. He greedily turned over onto her stomach and pushed his overbearing strong erection inside her.

"Hmmmm, okay," she assured with a gracious moan. ABL was charged up while he fervently took notice of his forward and outward sexual movement. His dick was saturated with the glossy coat of her enjoyment, and he loved the effects of her remarkable ass joyously bouncing off his pelvis and thighs. So in tune with his sense of endearment, ABL pressed her body into a forming arch to excite his visual allure. Adoring his ability, she attempted to push herself up, wriggling beneath his strength, just to feed his urge. The crave of it all was enticing. ABL pinned her in place, leaning forward with his weight on her back and wrapping his arm around her neck, constricting Jessica's air passage remotely while short jabbing her pussy with a persistent rhythm.

Jessica surely honored his from the back, since doggy style was her favorite and most desired position. ABL felt so large inside her that Jessica forfeited her strive to play against his semiaggressive behavior. She just lay there withstanding everything he had to offer. Her moans were explosive, ABL's drive was magnifying, and her body shifted with his movement. Jessica had no space to depress from his magnitude. His majestic force held her attention. She was enthralled by the flesh of this man. Her incitement was contested by his need, her continence of his desire. Her want was contiguous to the touch, even a mere glance of each other. It was all so challenging. Seemingly not only did ABL have authority of her physically, but also she was at a mental misconception for he stimulated her mind. She became highly addicted. Often she felt lost whenever he wasn't near, and she would get wet just from the thought of him. Her fingers would usually ease up her thigh from the anticipation of his arrival. Her thoughts flurried with the assemblage of creativity, the ideas and images of him, when her brain ticked of his surge. She was embedded in his embrace, as he thrived to praise Jessica's sensation. She rumbled within her speech. Her eyes were sealed tight, and she felt his warm breath at the back of her neck, as he moved her hair to the side. A gentle peck was placed at the base of her neckline, a tingle that shook her body like a cold chill.

ABL was finally at his breaking point. His erection was suddenly feeling like an eruption. That thick vein protruded like an overbearing muscle. Before he realized it, he found himself bursting a massive load all over her back, while he ejaculated his dick to a flimsy halt. Jessica just loved it when he would cum all over her. She replenished her version, slightly looking back at him, simply offering a blissful smile.

# CHAPTER 22

"Babe, wake up!" Jessica nudged ABL while he appeared to be at ease within his sleep, later that evening. At the touch, he became startled, quickly swinging his feet from the couch to the floor. His eyes earnestly peered in every direction of the room, even overlooking Jessica, as she stood right in front of him, a bit rattled herself.

"What's up?" ABL's tone was elusive. He was slightly groggy.

"Here!" She handed him his phone. "This thing been going off back to back," Jessica sounded agitated.

ABL studied her expression, before receiving the phone from her grasp. Furtively he thought he cut it off, but of course the sex between him and Jessica knocked him off-balance. Then he suddenly realized he had a voice activation to unlock his screen.

"Why you got that look on your face?" he inquired, taking notice of her dominant expression.

"Babe, it's nothing," she insisted and then walked away.

"Naw, come here. Talking about nothing." He hopped up and dashed toward her. "What's wrong? F—— all that passive sh——. Talk!" ABL stood in her way, where she attempted to sidestep him, but he stepped with her. Jessica smacked her lips, before exhaling a heavy stream of air from her mouth.

"ABL, watch out, please." He simply remained in place. "I told you it was nothing." She tried again to bypass him.

"Your whole demeanor is telling me that it's something. It's only nothing because you don't want to talk about it," he stated matter-of-factly.

Jessica looked up, as she hindered her urge to smile. She wasn't even really mad at him. It was all just an illusion, only because he hasn't come forward about his sly dealings. So Jessica figured this would be the best time to pry, and hopefully he will get caught up in a lie, as most men do.

"I'm trying to understand why your phone would be ringing like that. Who would be wanting to get in touch with you that urgently?" She awaited his response with her brows stuck between her eyes and her thick hip postured outward.

"Obviously, my phone is ringing because people are trying to get in touch with me. What you mean?"

"I know that, smart-ass." She rolled her eyes. "That ain't answering my question at all." She forcefully pushed past him and headed toward the kitchen. "Here goes the f——ing games," she shouted over her shoulder.

ABL was on her heels, gently but flagrantly grabbing her arm, ceasing Jessica in her tracks. "Whoa, whoa. Hold up. Okay, listen!" He hesitated. "I'm just networking, baby. You know, meeting people. Simply trying to prove a way," ABL said.

"ABL, what you mean networking? What was wrong with my contacts?" Jessica asked with a stern expression.

"They were cool. But $10 an hour and taking orders just isn't what I'm into."

"Excuse me." Jessica snapped her neck hard enough to cause her long hair to fling over her shoulder. "I put my name on that sh——. Are you serious?" The two were now at an intense stare off. No sound ensued. No movement occurred between them.

ABL's mind raced with what to actually say, thinking where she was coming from, and Jessica was itching for him to reply as she expected him to. Instead of a verbal back and forth display of fury—because usually an argument is nothing more than two people fighting to get their point across at the sometime, one overtalking the other or the other simply just yelling, shouting, cussing, and fussing and this was an aspect of life ABL didn't have the patience to entertain and one thing he knew about women if nothing else was that they were always right—he more or less flashed a smile of defeat, leaned in, and gave Jessica a peck on her lips. Without allowing anything negative to surface further in her mind, ABL swiftly disappeared upstairs. He found a seat along the side of the bed and activated his screen on his cellphone. He had twenty missed calls and six missed text messages. One of the six messages was from Yazmine, which read, "Meet me tonight at eight. Same place we met." Another one was from Caroline, "R we hooking up 2nite? I got a room over here by the airport." ABL nodded his head, a sly grin appearing on his face, before he headed toward the bathroom, completely disregarding the rest of his messages.

Meanwhile, Jessica stood facing her neatly manicured lawn, the landscaping elegantly stylish. It was 7:25 p.m., and the day's humidity turned into a placid breeze. The window was slightly open, and she favorably inhaled the scent of the freshly cut grass, as the coolness blew at her skin. Jessica certainly was missing Florida, and while thoughts ran rampant back and forth, there were so many things she couldn't place her mind to, haunting things that often prevented her sleep. Then there was this Julio guy. If only she had taken Kevin Winsten's advice on the notion that people are not who you always expect them to be, then just maybe she would have had a more peaceful mind, though that's never a thought of action, as it's said, "Nobody said life would be fair. It was always told to be worth it."

Jessica railed all the possibilities, which even had her looking at her man in a certain kind of way, which should never be cast upon the man she claimed to love. "Antonio Demarco," she thought out loud, as if to remind herself there's no one to be trusted in this gamble. It's one thing to lust over someone, but it's another to actually love someone and commit all of your trust and faith into that one person. Jessica puzzled over the idea; she grappled at the sense of it all. Then there was concept of how things would pan out between her and Luca Gussalli. Sure, she understood with all the bloodshed and strife with the Lopez brothers. It really didn't have the option to be any other way.

It was as if her back was against the wall. She felt like she was being attacked from all angles with nowhere to go and no one to turn to. Her hands felt as if they were bound with barbwire. She was helpless. Everything she strived for seemed to be lost. Her father's honor was depleted. The name she carried in favor of that man was now nothing more than a billboard of disappointment read within her solemn expression. Scenes of things in what they used to be came and went like a heaving dream.

Jessica's eyes were filled with tears, but before one of them could even escape, ABL appeared like the sun peeking through the clouds on a gloomy day. He simply stared at her for a moment, feeling her out more or less. Comfortably he reached for her hand. Jessica's first thought was to reject his touch, but it was all too tempting. He pulled her away from her menacing stance and out of her looming train of thought and into his warm embrace. Her head rested peacefully on his chest. Her arms looped around his waist, while he rocked with her from side to side. Whatever it was that he appeared to be saying, Jessica wasn't paying any attention. She felt good, and she assumed she was about to melt. His strength, his smell, and just him, period, caused Jessica to forget everything that was going on or whatever that may had happen. She was in a different state of mind whenever ABL presented himself. Jessica closed her eyes and allowed herself to enter a place in her heart she rarely ever visited, a place humans tend to conceal their most desired emotions. And there it was, a stream of tears spilled from her eyelids.

# CHAPTER 23

ABL decided to focus more of his attention on Jessica. He felt like he was neglecting their relationship. Slowly he was exposing his hand, and he noticed Jessica wasn't as green as he thought. So ABL linked Yazmine and Caroline for the purpose of his distribution. He still maintained his vision, but this time, it was different. It was more agonizing without the third eye of his man Po. His little brother's absence still impaired his judgment. His sister Khari was still missing, either voluntary or involuntary. He just didn't know what to think.

ABL was unaware of his father's murder. Actually, ABL and his father haven't been on the best of terms since that New York hit, the one Detective Winsten orchestrated.

*****

"Take a good look at this photo," Detective Winsten insisted. He placed the picture in front of a young ABL and his friend Po. "This is the man I need y'all to take out." The pair observed the photograph impassively.

"But I'm saying, Pops, why us?" ABL asked, as he looked toward his friend. "We don't even know anything about New York to be out here running down on a nigga," he added, seeming slightly discombobulated.

"My point exactly. Y'all don't know anything about New York, and New York don't know anything about y'all," the detective explained. "That's the sole reason why I chose y'all two. It's giving y'all the advantage to do the damn thing and flee back to Ohio. There's nothing here linking y'all to New York. Y'all be like ghost."

"What's in it for us?" Po spoke up.

"A hundred grand apiece," Detective Winsten replied.

ABL and Po glanced at each other with appeasement. The detective took heed of their nonverbal agreement and casually continued. "Tomorrow afternoon, he will be at an ice cream shop in Manhattan. He will be accompanied by his lovely wife, but the contract is strictly for him." Detective Winsten glared at his son, before shifting his stern expression toward Po. "Is this understood?"

ABL and Po solemnly agreed.

"Good," he said. He reached beneath the table the three occupied within a small Brooklyn apartment and retrieved two revolvers with attached silencers from a brown paper bag. "Here." He handed Po and ABL each a pistol. "We won't make this any harder than it needs to be. ABL, I want you to walk up behind him and put one in the back of his head. Po, you will seal the deal by putting two in his chest. Afterward, y'all will calmly walk eastbound until you see a white Mercury parked on the opposite side of the street. The key will be stashed above the driver's side rear tire. Drive two blocks over, and there will be a black Lincoln Town Car sitting up the street from Saks Fifth Avenue. Take that car to JFK International. Y'all's plane tickets will be inside the glove compartment, which y'all will stash those pistols in and leave the keys in the ignition. The two of you will receive the payment of two hundred grand once you touch down in Columbus."

"All right, bet, Pops." ABL grinned. Po just nodded his head, as he stared attentively. "But, hey, I got to ask. What's in it for you?" ABL looked skeptically at his father.

"Position, son," the detective replied. "Life is all about positioning yourself. Always remember that."

*****

Just another typical day in the streets of Columbus. ABL and Jessica cruised through the city in Jessica's pumpkin orange 2015 BMW Convertible. The two enjoyably spent their day shopping, eating, and spa bathing. They were simply lost in each other's company. ABL was even holding her hand, as he navigated through the congestion of traffic, a warming touch of the two. She gazed tenderly.

"Would you just look at this bitch?" one of the Lopez brothers expressed antagonistically. "She thought running to Ohio was going to be her plan in avoiding her death sentence." He smirked from behind the steering wheel. He sipped his Pepsi, before glancing over at his brother, who reclined low in his seat with an implacable look, as he cherished the AR-10 assault rifle that rested between his legs. He held firm control of it anxiously, as if he was ready to hang out the window and let it rip right there in traffic. The brother driving kept a close eye on his brother's unpredictable behavior. He began to fiddle with the switch that converted the rifle from semi- to fully automatic, and he commenced to strain his words within a rant of Spanish. His eyes was looming, his body tense.

"I know it feels like we've been following this bitch all day." The brother finally spoke through a mouth full of chewing tobacco. "I'm tired of this cat-and-mouse b——." He picked up an empty 20 oz. Mountain Dew bottle, rolling around on the floor of the Dodge Ram 1500 beneath his feet, and spit the tobacco residue inside it. "Let's just kill this bitch right here, right now." He looked at his elaborate timepiece. "We'll make it back to Florida before supper," the man declared. "Just pull up, and I'll take care of it." He adjusted the weapon in his grasp.

"Timing, my friend. It's all about presenting yourself at the right time," the brother responded.

Suddenly, the BMW came to a halt at a red light on North High Street. Jessica just so happened to peer in the rearview mirror, applying a new coat of lip gloss to her already lustrous lips. "What the f——," Jessica said, noticing the Lopez brothers a car behind her. At first she assumed she was hallucinating.

ABL was so caught up in his smugness that he didn't pay attention to Jessica easing the all-pink 9 mm Glock from under her seat. "Julio," she muttered. Quickly, she drew her attention over her shoulder. She squinted, still unable to believe her eyes. A funny feeling consumed her instantly.

"She made us!" the brother roared.

"Go! Go! Go!" Jessica yelled once the passenger side door swung open, frantically hitting ABL's arm.

"Huh? What? Go where?" He appeared puzzled. "Do you not see this car in front of us?" ABL glanced over at Jessica. The boisterous sound from the first shot, steaming from the extension of her arm, caused ABL to duck in his seat.

She resumed firing shots into the door the brother disappeared to hide behind. Her arm weaved accurately across the windshield. Jessica's posture was planted firmly in the vehicle. "Let's go!" she continued to shout.

The other brother took cover, stabilizing himself underneath the dashboard. Slugs relentlessly tore through its interior, as tiny specks of glass dispersed like confetti.

ABL slammed the gearshift into reverse, flooring the pedal, and smashing the $60,000 automobile into the car behind them. Jessica tumbled within the back seat upon impact, bringing her barrage of gunfire to a cease. Hastily, ABL threw the gearshift back in drive, cutting the steering wheel toward the open lane.

Within a split second, the Lopez brother sprang into action, emerging from behind the bullet-riddled door and briskly moving across the pavement, allowing a sequence of rounds to entrench the body of the BMW. ABL's quick eye spotted his advantage. He rolled out from the driver seat, staying low to the ground. He pulled his 9 mm from his waistline and locked eyes with the other brother, catching him by surprise, as he stared out from the bullet hole that obscured his vision. ABL lifted his pistol and shot blindly, yet hitting the man in the ear, momentarily silencing the streets. ABL suddenly popped up from between the car and Dodge Ram 1500, just as the other brother was advancing on the BMW. Unaware of his presence, ABL was able to sneak up behind him. Shoving the gun to the back of his head, a petrified spark read in his eyes.

"Hey, release that m—— gun, dude," ABL demanded.

At the sound of his voice, Jessica peeked out from the back seat. "No!" she shouted. The panic in her voice was evident. "Leave him. Let's go." Jessica crawled between the seats, settling within the driver seat, and pulled into the open lane. "I said leave him," Jessica insisted.

"And I said release that m—— gun, dude," ABL repeated himself. Pressing the gun even harder to his head, he demanded, "Don't make me say it again."

"I think you better listen to the bitch." He laughed. "This is way out of your league, nigger boy."

"What you just say?" he spoke through clenched teeth. Before another word came to mind, ABL simply pulled the trigger, dropping the brother right there in broad daylight.

Everyone outside pointed and stared. Shock was the only word to define their expression, as the BMW sped off. ABL was furious, while they raced down the street, quickly turning off on Spruce Avenue and parking behind a taco shop, as the rushing sound of sirens wailed nearby.

"ABL, what the f—— was that?" Jessica's tone was amplified.

"You tell me what the f—— that was!" ABL's tone matched hers.

"You just gunned a man down in front of a hundred so witnesses. Are you serious? What the f—— was you thinking? Where did you get a gun anyway?"

"F—— where I got it from. Dude was trying to kill us," ABL replied, as he nervously looked over his shoulders.

"Okay, but I have men for that. That's not your position," she said. "Your sole position is to be my man. I don't need you to be out here trying to be my knight in shining armor." Jessica sighed softly.

"I'm not out here trying to be your knight or whatever that dumb sh—— you just said. I was just simply protecting us, what any real nigga would do. You talking about you got men for that." He paused. "There's something you ain't telling me." ABL looked over at her.

"What are you talking about?" she inquired. "Please don't try to make this about me. You f——ed up." Jessica firmly flung her finger in his direction.

"You got a team of armed, marine-looking m——s who watch your every move. Then you just had a cat trying to box you in the middle of the street, with all things a f——ing assault rifle. You came up here from Florida already taking a bullet in the shoulder. Baby, I'm a street nigga before anything. I know when there more than what a person is saying. You got personal drivers and sh——, living in a f——ing mansion, driving expensive-ass whips, and hella stacks of cash on deck. Do I look stupid or something?" His face frowned.

"You thinking too much into things that's not even relevant. Did you forget that you just killed a man? Let's talk about how you expect me to explain that."

"Yeah, of course. Explain to me why my girl is rolling around with a pink Glock under her seat. Explain to me why my model girlfriend was almost just executed." ABL left a guilt of silence to settle between them.

Jessica couldn't even look his way. She just graced her fingers through her hair and stared aimlessly out the windshield. She knew what he was getting at. She understood this conversation was bound to take place. There's only so much one could hide from another and only so much one could put into a lie, before he or she find his or her very own lie catching up with them.

# CHAPTER 24

Yazmine and Caroline just finished counting a quarter million in diminutive bills and wrapped each $5,000 bundles with rubber bands, as Talib Kweli played in the background of ABL's grandmother's house in his old neighborhood. Yazmine slouched in her seat, exhaling tediously. Caroline stood up and stretched her body, yawning, as fatigue settled in. ABL lingered at a distance, peeking back and forth from watching the series of *El Chapo* on Netflix to observing the movement outside.

"What's on your mind?" Yazmine asked within a whisper, as she gingerly approached him.

"Everything." He looked at her sincerely. "What made you ask?"

"I see it." She caressed his arm.

"Damn! It's that obvious." He struggled to smirk. "It's like you live through the worse and pray for the best. For every obstacle a nigga overcomes, there's always a new challenge around every corner. I'm just weighing out my options. It ain't nothing, doe." ABL dismissed her concern.

"Well, I'm here if you need anyone to listen," Yazmine offered. "What now?" She changed the topic. "The count was good," she added. She waited eagerly while devotedly staring at ABL. His expression was just empty. Yazmine could tell he was in search of something.

ABL knew his movement was slightly limited, and due to the heat in the streets, he was now living for the movement. "We wait," he said with a shrug of his shoulders. "Things are hot right now. We must be able to dance to the same tune and react off the same accord. If we move offbeat, something is likely to happen that we don't want to happen."

Just as ABL's words trailed off, the front door came crashing in, which ultimately caused ABL, Yazmine, and Caroline to scramble fearfully, only to halt in their tracks when two shots accommodated their apprehensiveness. A hollow-tip slug propelled through the kneecap of Yazmine and Caroline, sending them crumbling to the floor and screaming dreadfully. ABL scampered toward his pistol, but a striking blow was delivered to the back of his head. He staggered dizzily. Then the man raised his assault rifle again, ready to hit ABL with another blustering blow, until ABL found himself collapsing to the floor.

Everything seemed to happen so fast. He couldn't make anything out other than the whimpering sound of Yazmine and Caroline squirming on the floor and repulsively bleeding. Through the chaos and brief exchange of foreign words, the men became quiet. As ABL struggled to form a clear vision, slowly overcoming his haze, he noticed one of the men pacing while slightly stepping away from his partner. Worry built up on ABL's expression. The heavy expulsion of air heaved uncontrollably from his chest. Uncertainty shifted within his eyes, wandering cowardly. His head was throbbing painfully, as he scanned the entirety of the room. He was strategically thinking, as he felt the warm blood begin to trickle down his back. His gun was right there, exposed on the glass table, amidst a box of Twinkies, a pack of Twizzlers, and a pile of exotic buds next to a pack of Backwoods. His mind was racing. ABL wanted to go for it. He gambled with the thought tenaciously.

Suddenly, the man who eased away was back, whispering in the other man's ear, who displayed a distraught look upon his mug. They gazed intently at ABL. The two men angled their bodies, their knees slightly bent and their rifles extended, aimed directly at ABL's head. Their eyes beamed with rage. *What the f——?* were the only words his mind could formulate through a rambling mumble. ABL suddenly appeared glued to the floor. He couldn't move a limb. He was stuck, transfixed upon the men who were slowly nearing. Their barrels only inches away from his forehead, he could smell the burned powder of gun residue and charred metal. *These are killers indeed!* he thought. He just watched, waited, and listened. The persistent pulsation of his heart progressed to an echo, and he simply closed his eyes and accepted his fate, accepted the darkness from behind his eyelids as his mortal departure. The images that flashed were seemingly unbearable. Everything was disturbing his mind all at once. What ABL couldn't form a clear thought on was, *How the f—— did these Spanish m——s get the drop on a nigga?* They were perfect in their movement, a little too precise for just an ordinary hood robbery. *F—— a robbery!* ABL screamed in his mind. The army-style weapons formed too vividly. *These cats are out for blood*, he reassured himself, as the situation of the dude he shot down in the street suddenly intruded his recollection.

"ABL," a whisper sounded, snapping him back to reality. Confusion settled. It was as if he was dreaming. *Where is the barrage of gunfire?*" he asked himself. *These fettuccine-Alfredo-eating m——s even know my name. They toying with a nigga*, ABL added subconsciously.

"ABL!" the voice announced again, yet a notch louder. Startled, he instinctively moved backward on his hands, palms to the floor, scooting his ass across the carpet, until his back clashed against the wall. ABL quickly adjusted his eyes, sweat visibly saturating his skin, and there stood Khari Blade. She attempted to smile, but she trembled like a wet dog. Despite the hot climate, her teeth chattered, and her lips lightly quivered. Her once beautiful face ABL has always known her for was covered in sores.

"Bruh, what the f—— happened?" Khari managed to utter. While tiptoeing through the living room, ABL disregarded anything she had said. This was his little sister he was staring at, but he became completely speechless. It was shameful to finally have seen her, to see her like this. He appeared to be looking at a stranger. He instantly became emotionally torn, once he recognized that childish gleam from her eyes. She usually would reflect upon his gaze whenever she felt guilty about something. He heard the absurd murmur of Yazmine and Caroline, but he ignored it, just as much as he ignored his own pain, besides the infliction of pain that deceives him at this very moment.

Khari seemed to look at her brother strangely. Coming to their grandma's house, she didn't expect to bump into ABL. She haven't slept in days, let alone showered nor ate a proper meal. Khari knew she looked like a walking disgrace. The hurt was clearly seen on his expression. Khari wanted to just throw herself into ABL's arms. She missed him dearly. She needed that soothing sensation from a familiar touch. ABL bounced to his feet, fixed his clothing, brushed himself off, and smoothed out the little scuff mark on the suede of his Timberlands. He looked to his sister one last time, searching for something to say, but it just wasn't there. He simply cut his eyes from her and snatched up the TEC-9 off the table, clutching it at his side. He walked right past Khari toward the threshold where the door once stood, before being kicked off the hinges. ABL was completely in a daze. He just stared.

# CHAPTER 25

## *Flashback*

"Hey, Julio," Devecchio called out, as he walked up 125th Street. Julio spun around quickly. His hand was reaching underneath his Fubu garment. Devecchio simply smiled. He was up on Julio faster than Julio could even react. Devecchio gripped Julio's reaching advance. "Stand down, killer," Devecchio whispered. "Who's your friend here?"

"That's my Gray Daz Juan," Julio responded.

"Is he cool?" Devecchio inquired.

"Of course, yo," Julio replied with a smile of his own. "He with me, ain't he?" Devecchio released his hand. "What's up, yo? What you doing out here prowling?" The two men laughed.

"Actually, I'm out here to ask you a question," Devecchio replied.

"Ask a question?" Julio seemed surprised. "That's unusual." He laughed slightly. "But what's up, doe?"

"I need to find a Jessica McCray. Have you ever heard of her?" Devecchio asked behind a stern expression.

"Jessica," Julio mumbled. He rubbed at his chin, as he stared blankly toward the sidewalk. "I can't say I have," Julio lied. "Who is she?"

"Remember about a year ago, there was a double homicide in Manhattan that the news reported as a mob hit?" Devecchio said.

Julio glanced around. Finally, his stare met Daz Juan's before shifting his eyes back to Devecchio.

"Yeah, yeah." Julio nodded his head. "You talking about that kingpin cat." Julio repeatedly tapped Daz Juan's chest with the back of his hand. "Yo, the Dominican cat, b. He was selling bricks for dumb cheap." Julio became excessive in his demeanor. Daz Juan produced a coy smile but remained silent. "Yeah, I heard the streets went dry for months once he got whacked, yo. What about it?" Julio said.

"Jessica McCray is his daughter. Before he was killed, he gave me a few things to give to her," Devecchio replied. "I'm asking you because you got a longer reach in the streets with this generation."

"Yo, I can ask around," Julio suggested. "Just out of curiosity, doe. What is it that you trying to give to shorty? You know, in case I bump into her, yo," Julio urged.

"From how it was explained to me, Fernando knew he was going to be murdered. So he told me if it were to happen, I would give these things to his daughter, I guess which will identify whoever killed him."

"Yo, that's mad crazy, B," Julio replied. He and Daz Juan exchanged a faint look, which Devecchio took notice of. "For a daughter, that will be a heavy burden to carry." Julio eyed Devecchio. "Why not just leave it alone yo?"

"I gave the man my word, and as a man, I must honor my word. That's the only reason I'm putting forth any effort toward this situation," Devecchio responded.

"Yo, I got to respect a man who honors his word. Scarface said it best, 'All you got in this world is your balls and your word. And you don't break that for no one,'" Julio recited in his best Scarface voice. Devecchio just looked at him absurdly. "Who else did you mention this to?" Julio redeemed himself.

"Nobody really." Devecchio showed a wary expression. He felt something was off. Julio was giving off a strange vibe. "Maybe you are right. I should just leave it alone," he said.

"That just might be a good idea," Julio stated. "The news did disclose it to be a mob hit. Looking too hard for something that ain't meant to be found, you'll likely discover something else. Yo, you's an assassin. You know how this sh—— go."

"Yeah, I think I do," Devecchio replied. "Hey, just forget about it." He smirked. "You boys be easy." Devecchio gave Julio a soft pat on his back.

"No doubt, yo," Julio said. Just as Devecchio commenced to walk away, Julio looked toward Daz Juan. "What the f—— was that?" His face was twisted and confused. He glancing back up the street until Devecchio disappeared around the corner. "Hey, yo follow that m——. Keep a close eye on him, until I tell you something else. But yo play it smart as I said, dude is a real-life assassin for the mafia. He ain't no dummy."

"Say no more." Daz Juan jagged across the street. Julio thought for a moment. He wanted to stop Daz Juan, but he couldn't allow Devecchio to find Jessica. He quickly walked over to a pay phone on the side of an appliance store and dug in his pocket. He sifted through his change and came up with a quarter. After inserting the necessary change, he punched in the ten-digit number. A man's voice announced lazily.

"Hey, you what's up, B?" Julio spoke softly.

"What can I do for you, Julio?" the man replied.

"Yo, I think we got a problem," Julio insisted. "Can we meet up?"

"It ain't nothing you can handle." The man yawned into the phone. "And can you simply explain it to me first thing in the morning?"

"I don't think this is something that can wait." The phone went silent. "Yo, you want to hear this, trust me!"

"Look, Julio. I'm tired. I had two days of no rest. I'm backed up on cases." He yawned again. "Just give me the details." He sighed.

"Yo, Devecchio came by looking for Jessica." Julio paused. "He said he had something to give her, something from her father that possibly can lead to the arrest of his killers. As a homicide detective, I figured this would be a conversation you would be more than interested in." All Julio could hear on the other end was breathing. Seconds went by. "Yo, hello."

"Where are you?" Detective Winsten asked. His tone was shallow, though shaky, as tension began to strain in his voice.

"I'm on 125th Street, at Mario's Appliances," Julio answered.

"I'll be there in fifteen minutes," the detective said.

# CHAPTER 26

The beautiful bronze complexion of Jessica McCray shined so remarkably. The sun carelessly beamed off her radiant skin. She sat quietly with a perfect posture, far away from the city limit, somewhere on an isolated riverside. She held her head high, expressing her long neck and defined jawline. Her eyes were like diamonds, uncut and vibrant. She smelled of scented roses, appearing dreamily to the eye. She listened courteously, intently, and thoughtful to the very end.

"Jess, they must have followed me." Julio's voice trembled. His hands and feet were bound with chicken wire. His face was bruised and bloody from the violent beating Jessica's henchman laid upon him. Standing firmly behind Julio was her lieutenant with a blood-smeared baseball bat dangling at his side. "I swear to God, Jess," Julio pleaded. "If I was going to do some sh—— like that, why all of a sudden? Why now, Jess, when I had all the opportunity in the world to betray you, yo?"

"I don't know why people do half the things they do. But they do them," Jessica spoke calmly. "Julio, you been playing your hand hella f——ed up." She giggled. "I hate a person who isn't who they say they are." Julio strained his one eye over toward Jessica, as he grimaced in pain.

"Huh? What you mean?"

"You thought I wouldn't figure your punk-ass out?" She laughed. "The Sinaloa Cartel never heard of you. It's impossible for you to be connected with the Zetas. You even laid claim to a few murders that you didn't commit." Jessica removed that fraudulent smile from the face. She stared at Julio feeling completely numb.

"Yo, Jess, hold up. Wait a minute. You got things all wrong," Julio said.

Jessica stood up from the bank of the river, dusted her rear off, and slowly advanced on a helpless Julio. He coughed up blood. He twisted and turned on the ground. "I got things all wrong you say?" She loomed over him. "So what you know about Detective Winsten?"

"Detective who?" Julio said.

"Now you don't know who I'm talking about." Jessica looked at her lieutenant. She gave him a favorable eye. The man swung the bat high above his head and forcefully brought it down into Julio's already broken ribs. Julio wailed in agony. The feeling was excruciating. Julio's entire body was badly confused.

"I'm sure we are on the same page now, right?" Julio nodded his head. His face was stifled in the dirt. "Tell me your involvement with my parents' murder. And don't lie. Your testimony is the only thing that's keeping you alive."

"Okay, I'll tell you. Yo, just don't hit me again," he mumbled weakly. "It was all that detective's idea, B. Yo, he flew two cats in from here. Two Ohio cats, yo. One of 'em was his son, he mentioned."

"You said his son?" Jessica uttered with astonishment.

"My orders were to oversee the situation and make sure the job got done. Yo, I didn't pull the trigger. Yo, that's my word. Them Ohio cats killed your fam." Julio struggled to breathe. Every bone in his body felt like they were shattered. A sharp sensation pierced at his lung.

"I know that much. I want to know why. What was the reason?" Jessica squatted beside him.

"The detective assumed that he would have inherited your father's empire." Julio coughed strenuously. "He even guaranteed me a top spot within his organization. Yo, dude was on a power trip. He thrived off it. He would even complain about all the blood on his hands is what built your father's claim to fame. But, yo, he wasn't getting recognized as such."

"That doesn't even make any sense," Jessica responded. "So if this was all over a power trip, how did my mother get caught up in the envy of Detective Winsten?"

"Yo, that ain't how that was 'pose to go down. She was just at the wrong place at the wrong time, not to mention those Ohio cats got trigger-happy." Julio paused. He switched over to his other side. He groaned at the slightest shift of his body. "Besides, he was having an affair with your mother."

Jessica suddenly jolted to her feet. She looked at Julio confused. She was overwhelmed, though she wasn't surprised that her mother was cheating. Jessica just would have never thought it would have been with Detective Winsten. Her mother was sneaky and very much a woman who always got her way. Jessica walked back over to the bank of the river. She was in serious thought. "That explains a lot," she muttered. "And what about me?" She spun around.

"What about you?"

"What did he have in-store for me?"

"Nothing, yo," Julio said. "Nothing he ever told me."

"Yeah, but that doesn't say anything about you," Jessica declared. "What did you have in mind?" She switched her massive hips toward Julio once again. "You always seem to be thinking of something."

"Naw, Jess. It ain't even like that. Yo, I got mod respect for you." He winced. "I never thought like that toward you, yo."

"But you insist the Lopez Brothers followed you, just so haply." Jessica's tone was intense. "You must have been my leak the entire time. That's why they knew my every move, huh?" She laughed. "I should have never trusted you." She shook her head disgracefully. "Especially that move you pulled on me the night you killed Fabian. You just wanted me all to yourself. You sick son of a bitch. It was never about loyalty with you. What was I thinking?" she ranted. "You even killed your friends."

"I killed for you!" Julio blurted. Jessica plunged her foot into his chest, causing a large substance of blood to spew from his mouth.

"No!" she yelled. "You killed because you wanted to. I don't even know why I'm wasting my time." Jessica retrieved the .380 from the small of her back. Julio, unable to speak, moaned miserably. She stood over his body, extended her arm firmly toward his head, and opened fire, shooting Julio multiple times, scattering his brain tissue mercilessly. The small holes in his head and face slowly oozed of fluids. His body slightly jerked.

Jessica descended the smoking gun to her side, before turning away and disregarding her actions as if it was nothing. "Leave his body," she said to her lieutenant. "I need a message to be sent."

# CHAPTER 27

ABL and Jessica just finished having the hottest quickie since DMX f——ked that chocolate stallion of a woman in the movie *Belly*. It was steaming. Their body glisten with sweat. Both were exhausted. The enchanting aroma of sex dominated the human senses. He watched pleasantly as Jessica roamed throughout the bedroom, gathering up her discarded garments. ABL worked up another erection while fondling himself, looking at the wonderful jiggle of her scrumptious ass with every step. Jessica noticed him slowly stroking his dick from the corner of her eye. She smiled sheepishly.

"I don't even know why you over there hyping yourself up." She laughed. "That ain't what we agreed to." Yet she couldn't hinder her stare from ABL's hand artistically rotating around his massive dick. *OMG!* she thought, as her urge to wrap her mouth around it caused her teeth to bite down on her bottom lip. "Hmmm." Jessica amusedly embraced the lustful thought from her adventurous mind.

"Come here, baby," ABL insisted in a low sexy tone. "I ain't going to bite." He smirked.

"Yeah, but I might," she taunted. Her eyes beamed excitedly.

"One more time ain't never hurt anybody," he urged. "Just touch it," he teased. Jessica stalled for a moment admired by his sexual behavior. It was as if she was being induced by hypnosis of the dick. A small groan escaped from his parted lips. The mere sight of it was amazing. It was beautifully formed into one flawless piece of manly flesh. His pubic hairs were even trimmed perfectly.

"You going to leave me to handle this big m—— all by myself?" ABL removed his hand and placed it behind his head with the other, interlocking his fingers with anticipation of an ending with his cum shooting all over her face. Jessica was astounded at how stern his dick was after just busting a heavy load down the crack of her ass.

It has been two tedious weeks of them not being intimate with each other. After the murder of the infamous Lopez brother, Jessica insisted that ABL lay low, just until she felt it was safe, even though the situation for Jessica was more like a splinter in the thumb. She still had a billion-dollar operation to uphold, and now with this fentanyl becoming more popular, Jessica was looking to triple her net worth. Her connects were growing, and her orders were doubling. She was forming alliances and planting her seeds in new cities. Ohio started looking profitable.

Jessica's focus on ABL had been sort of bleak to say the least. She felt bad though, because this was the man she fell in love with, the man she promised forever and a day with. ABL had the ability to make Jessica feel different, feel whole, feel complete without the want or need of Gucci, Prada, and Burberry. ABL was crafted with heart and hard work, which made Jessica feel so at home within her soul, with the man who captivated her mind and body like a sorcerer. They would go to IHOP on the weekend, her usual order a toffee-apple-cheese-cake-stuffed French toast. She had been accustomed to this after ABL introduced it to her. Oftentimes Jessica would venture off by herself and take the more sensible approach with an order of pancakes, cheese eggs, and bacon along with four hot and spicy sausage links. It was a complete 360 from the usual five-star restaurants she spoiled herself with frequently over the years, where $500 plates were more reasonable than $10 for an entirely delicious and comforting meal. She felt free yet cheated in knowing that life had so much more to offer. Out of the billions of dollars she grossed, the lavish lifestyle she lived, and position of power she claimed, Jessica still limited herself.

"You better go put some ice on the genitals." Jessica playfully tossed a personalized towel in his direction. The towel landed right on the head of his dick, forming a pitched tent. To add insult to injury, she laughed.

"That's cold." He chuckled. "That's how we playing it?" He planted his feet onto the floor. Disappointment strained his features. His dick fell limp.

"I told you before you even came over I didn't have time to f—— around. We both said a quickie would do us some justice. Look"—Jessica examined her Chopard timepiece and smacked her lips—"I'm already three minutes late." She slipped on her thong panties and began to dress in a rush.

"We definitely don't want you to be late to your so-called meeting." His sarcasm was evident. "A modeling agency, right?" He smirked.

Unbeknownst to ABL, this particular meeting was the negotiation of a deal for five hundred kilograms of heroin with an all-white supremacy biker gang, settled within the rural parts of Ohio. She utilized her pipeline from Florida up through Dayton to a stash house in the plain city of Ohio.

"ABL, please! Let's not do this again. The sex was fantastic. I loved it. But this is where I need you to be mindful. You are not supposed to be here. And we ain't supposed to be together. We must keep in mind that man you killed still has a brother out there that's heavily connected."

"And? So the f—— what?" ABL became defensive. Jessica sighed annoyingly. "Like seriously, f——, dude. Niggas get killed every day," he yelled.

"That's your f——ing problem, ABL." She paused momentarily, as if she was second-guessing how she truly felt. "It's nothing," she spoke with a low tone.

"Naw, say what you got to say," ABL insisted. His demeanor was edgy.

"You just ain't paying attention." Jessica shifted her stare from her reflection in the mirror and looked toward ABL dauntlessly. "Niggas do get killed every day. But what you fail to realize is that dude was not a nigga. This isn't that type of situation where someone gets killed and people just turn the other cheek or simply plaster his face on a T-shirt. Some powerful people are going to be expecting answers behind what you did, and I'm going to be the one they come to for those answers."

"But you speaking on this dude as if he wasn't about to kill you, doe." ABL laced up his Air Max 95. "It's like you keep jumping to defend his actions and holding my actions against me. You haven't said thanks or good looking out, not one time."

"This is a whole different approach to what you may be used to. It's just you must get permission to kill certain people in life. It's not about a thank-you or showing a sense of gratitude. It's about knowing who's who." Jessica walked out of the room, leaving ABL speechless. One half of him felt disrespected. The other half reasoned with what she had to say. He had to be open-minded to the fact "only nigga's kill niggas." "Niggas don't kill mad men." ABL pondered over the thought, tucking his pistol in the waistline of his fitted AG jeans.

# CHAPTER 28

Three days advanced into another night. It was five to 10:00 p.m. on ABL's Louis Vuitton watch. He sat idle in a rusty old '96 Impala. Right next to him was his sister Khari Blade. Her first day out from a rehabilitation clinic, she sat nervously yet patiently with an SKS resting earnestly on her lap. A black ski mask concealed her features, as she caressed the minirifle with a daring spark in her eyes. Across the street, which held both ABL and Khari's attention, was a chicken and waffle diner on Livingston Avenue that closed well over an hour ago. ABL's vivid stare had been glued on the establishment since 8:00 p.m., upon their arrival. Neither really spoke much. They were more or less impaled.

"Bro, you sure this is the spot?" Khari whispered.

"Trust me, sis. This is it. There's the white Lexus truck that was even mentioned in the witness statements," ABL replied.

"And how many white Lexus trucks you think are in the city?"

ABL breathed heavily. He shifted in his seat.

"Yo, I'm just saying, bro. I want to be sure these are the same m——s that killed Po and our lil' bro," she reassured.

"Sis, I dropped fifty thousand in the street just for this information. I'm confident that's the only white Lexus truck in Columbus that matter," he said.

Suddenly, a black SUV pulled along the side of the Lexus truck. The rear door of the SUV opened, and a familiar figure emerged solely. The car became eerily quiet. Both ABL and Khari squinted forward. There was something there they both recognized equally.

"Hey, bro, that's the chick I was telling Po about." Khari tapped ABL hostilely on his arm.

"Huh? What chick, sis?" ABL felt queasy just from the mere mention of what his sister was referring to. "You told Po what?"

"That's the queenpin, chick, the daughter of that drug lord from New York." Khari removed her ski mask after sensing the awkwardness. She looked toward him. "You know, the daughter of the guy—"

"I know the guy you talking about," ABL quickly intervened. "Her name is Jessica. That's my bitch." His voice settled softly.

"As in your girlfriend?" Khari sounded shocked. "Like your Florida bitch? The one you knocked off in the joint?" Khari was taken aback. ABL's harsh suppression told Khari everything. "Yo, you can't be serious."

"How was I supposed to know?" ABL declared. "All I could go off is what she told me."

"I see we got a lot to talk about," Khari insisted. "But, hey, bro, if these m——s killed Po and Decarlo, what's her connection with these cats?" she inquired.

"That's what I'm over here thinking about," ABL replied.

"Well, bro, we got to think fast. They getting in the truck." Khari clutched the SKS, as the brake lights on the Lexus suddenly illuminated, along with the black SUV Jessica got back in. "I wonder what she just handed the dude, bro." She looked up and down the street.

"F—— it!" ABL shouted. "Let the bitch slide. We are going to catch back up with her."

Khari eased her ski mask back over her face. ABL adjusted his own ski mask, before tossing the hood over his head. The two rushed out from the car, with CAR-15 in hand. ABL stayed low. He and Khari quickly filled in the distance, their adrenalin pumping.

"Sis, stay on point," he said meekly.

ABL raised the CAR-15, and Khari followed suit. They opened fire, creating a terrifying sound. The muzzle flash sparked graphically. Shell casings dispelled rapidly as bullets penetrated the rear of the Lexus, as the black SUV that Jessica occupied recklessly took off backward. Cars came to a screeching halt, while the black SUV maneuvered up Livingston Avenue in reverse, swerving through traffic attempting to flee unscathed. ABL and Khari fired continuously, leaving an echo in the streets like the chopping melodies of helicopter propellers. Projectiles riddled the Lexus, ripping through seats and doors, as the entire truck rocked from each explosive impact. Each man inside suffered from multiple gunshots, fatally wounding all four men. Two silver chargers came racing around the corner, stopping abruptly on the foreground of ABL and Khari's raging terror. Quickly, they ran over to the awaiting vehicles, one driven by Caroline and the other by Yazmine. Once inside both cars, they sped off in separate directions.

*****

ABL entered Jessica's home later that evening. An hour after the deadly assault, he was desperately seeking answers. There was too much on his mind for him to consider everything a coincidence. The house was unusually dark. It was serene. Her army style of men was nowhere in sight. He had a weird feeling, so he paced gingerly. Jessica's alluring scent lingered in the air. A half glass of white wine sat next to her favorite Gucci handbag on the kitchen counter. Oddly, he peeked over his shoulders. Just then, he caught a glimpse of a silhouette, so he tried adjusting his eyes, before the voice became clear.

"So you are Kevin Winsten's son?" Jessica uttered. Slowly she stepped closer.

ABL noticed the shiny object in her hand, held at her side, which he made out as a pistol. ABL took a step back. Jessica didn't need him to answer what she already knew to be true. He was uncertain. He wanted to rush to her, though his reaction was timid.

Jessica laughed. "I knew who you were all along." She approached a little closer. "But that was a surprise. I didn't realize how close the detective was playing it." Jessica pointed the gun to his head. "Now I get to save the best for last." She marched ABL into the living room. A stern expression spoiled her features.

"Hey, what are you saying?" ABL's speech trembled. "Listen, it wasn't like that," he stressed. "I didn't know."

"You and your punk-ass friend killed my dad and mother." Jessica drew her arm back, smacking ABL swiftly across his face with the steel of her pistol. He stumbled. Blood commenced to trickle down his skin. He was delirious, as he fought to maintain his equilibrium. "So I guess the death of your brother and father were a fair exchange," Jessica announced.

ABL looked at her fatuously. His eyes were disheartened. He couldn't believe what he was hearing, though there was nothing he could say. Even with the pain weighing within his heart, he couldn't lash out emotionally, as he wanted to.

"It was business," ABL mumbled. "I was young. My pops hit me with an offer I couldn't refuse. I didn't ask any questions. We just did it," ABL said. Jessica stood there with her gun trained on him. "But that doesn't determine what I felt toward you."

Jessica laughed. "I don't give a f—— about none of that!" she insisted firmly. "This isn't about what you can say to talk your way out of it. I have waited fifteen years to avenge the death of my parents. You really think anything you say will change my mind?"

ABL simply dropped his head in defeat.

"Even though killing you would be too easy." Jessica's arm hung back to her side. She took a few steps back. "I got something else planned for you." She flung her hair from her face. A wicked grin emerged.

ABL was stuck. His hand caressed his seeping wound right below his eye. He didn't know what to say. Any man in the world would love and cherish an opportunity to embrace such a moment, straight off a fifteen-year sentence at that. Jessica was rich and powerful. Right now, this is a lesson ABL didn't measure up as to be in his favor. What's done in the dark would soon find its way to the light. Sometimes too much of the wrong thing could turn a good thing disastrous, and not enough of both could make something so complicated. ABL just looked at her, lost in her stare, searching the pain hidden behind her strength, thinking about what he could possibly say to hinder his mistakes to make right with a woman through a sense of words, even when he knew he ain't living right. Often people always let us know who they are, but we are not listening.

"So why even f—— me then?" ABL now stood firm. His shoulders were squared. He cockily placed his hands over his pelvis, one hand over the other. "You can't tell me that ain't mean sh—— to you."

"Some dick?" Jessica frowned. "I f——ed you because I wanted to. Do I look like I'm a woman who needs anything from a man?" She smirked. "You can't be serious," Jessica spoke mildly.

Suddenly, a foul odor attacked ABL's sense of smell. It was a smell he knew all too well. He glanced over the dark room. He noticed a few things scattered about, things that struck ABL oddly. Jessica was known for her compulsive behavior. The disarray of the room was confusing, not to mention the pungent stench he was enduring. He looked around farther, straining as he squinted. Approaching the middle of the room, he felt something soggy beneath his shoes. Jessica hit the light switch, bringing forth the sight of pure evil. Bloody limbs were strewed everywhere. Blood was smeared and settled within the entirety of the room. ABL's eyes bulged from his skull. The severed heads of Caroline and Yazmine sat on each arm of the sofa facing him. Their eyes were open wide, as the horrid expression was left upon their face. Abruptly, Agent Pisaro appeared from the shadows, dousing ABL with a bucket of blood. Simultaneously he pulled his service weapon from his hostler. ABL was mortified. All he could do was look at his saturated clothing, as the warmth of the substance blotted his skin.

"Freeze!" Agent Pisaro shouted. "Keep your hands where I can see them." He slowly approached ABL. "Turn around," Agent Pisaro instructed. ABL reluctantly did as he was told and at the same time he stared fiercely at Jessica. Pisaro sternly grabbed ABL's wrist, forcefully twisting his arm behind his back. "You have the right to remain silent." Agent Pisaro slapped the handcuffs on his wrist, as he continued to read ABL his rights.

"Jessica, what the f—— is this?" ABL disputed. "Under arrest for what?" he shouted over his shoulder to Agent Pisaro. "And, dude, what you throw all this blood on me for?"

"You are under arrest for the murder of Caroline Pankow and Yazmine Joplin," Pisaro insisted.

"Say what? Hell naw, I ain't kill them." ABL tried to tug away from the overly tense agent. "Y'all can't put this on me."

Jessica laughed. "With your record, what makes you think we can't?" She continued to display her humor. "A credible witness, and DNA never lies. I told you killing you would be too easy. I rather you suffer in prison for the rest of your life," she said.

"How can you hold something against me I wasn't aware of? Besides, a woman in your position, I'm sure you have had your share of murders either personally or through the hands of your hired goons." ABL studied Jessica's expression. "What makes you any different from me?"

# THE LAST CHAPTER

ABL was booked into Franklin County Jail on two counts of aggravated murder. A few months after that, he was indicted on another murder charge, the murder of Carlos Lopez. ABL's hope was destroyed. They even had the gun, to no surprise. ABL paced back and forth from the wall to the bars. He couldn't believe Jessica played her hand so strategically. He was being held with no bond due to the seriousness of the crime. It was almost 5:00 p.m., and again Khari failed to come and visit her brother, as he needed her to. ABL was in need of a good lawyer. He had $200,000 stashed in the floor of an old abandoned duplex, across the street from his grandma's house, though he didn't have anybody to call on. The whole situation looked grim. He felt hurt and betrayed, yet he didn't allow it to show. ABL maintained his strength, thinking one man's luck couldn't be that bad. He shuffled within his thoughts. His father crossed his mind. His brother crossed his mind. Every decision he made upon his release crossed his mind. ABL even reconsidered his dreams and goals. That was four years ago. ABL was back at RCI doing triple life.

"So what happened to the Jessica chick?" ABL's cellmate asked, more than intrigued with the story of ABL's life, as he sat on his top rack rolling a joint with Bible paper.

ABL paced the concrete floor. A dunce expression rattled his mug. He looked over at the wall. ABL's cellmate had a variety of sexy, half-naked, curvaceous women, ripped from the pages of *Bottles N Modelz*, *I Adore*, and *Thick* magazines, plastered to the wall with toothpaste in a lusty decoration.

"Sh——, bro, there she goes." ABL pointed to a specific picture.

"Huh? Where?" ABL's cellmate sounded surprised. His eyes seemed to have deceived him. "Bro, stop playing." He chuckled.

"You talking about the bitch with Miz Davenport?" ABL just looked at him seriously. "Damn!" the cellmate uttered. "She really started modeling, huh?"

"Man, I lost so much in the process of f———ing with that bitch. I could care less what she out there doing," ABL said. He snatched the picture off the wall and balled it up before tossing it in the toilet. "F—— that bitch! I got to get my life back or take that bitch's life." ABL stared out the window toward the razor wire. "I can't let this be the end of my story. Straight up!" His voice lowered. His forehead was pressed to the bars.

ABL was bitter, and his sentence was stressing him overwhelmingly. His face aged. His hair was thinning. His weight was slender. He was now in deep thought. He couldn't even pick up the phone and call anybody. The only time he made it to commissary was with $17 (state pay) once a month. His JPay never revealed any new messages. ABL was all alone. He was just the man on the streets with nothing but a story to tell. He had nothing but a memory of how life used to be as his soul wept. His days were long. His nights were restless.

"My nigga, I know it ain't my place to say. But through whatever we encounter, bro, life is life. We got to stay positive and allow our past to be our past," ABL's cellmate insisted. His feet dangled from the side of his rack. ABL's vibe was suddenly off. His energy felt subsided. "I can tell there's a lot that still trouble you. Bro, you got a lot of pain trapped behind your eyes. Not trying to be funny, but you got to learn how to accept what you can't change and plan forward."

ABL spun around with a smirk. "That's easy for you to say. You got like forty-eight hours to the gate." ABL laughed. He walked to his cell door and peered out the narrow-sized window. He noticed a female corrections officer at the desk, congregating with other officers. Standing with her back facing ABL's direction, her pants snugged to her lower extremity, your typical-looking white chick. But she possessed a protruding physique, not fat, but fit her posture. Her hips were wide, and her thighs were full of substance. Her ass was plump and bulky, and her expression was always stern, but she was worth looking at to get a nigga through those lonely nights, simply fantasizing.

"Look at Ms. Shoemaker's thick ass," ABL said. "See, this is my life." He turned to face his cellmate. "I'm stuck with thoughts like that, jacking my dick to bitches I only wish to f——." ABL shook his head. "That's some creepy sh——. Bro, there's nothing for me to look forward to. I don't have any family out there. I lost it all. I even feel like I'm losing a piece of myself. Bro, on some real sh——, I don't even look at days as the next nigga do. Sometimes I don't feel like I exist. If you could travel in my mind and see what I be thinking, you'll know exactly what I mean."

"I say use your experience and this time of doing nothing to do something. Sitting here harboring feelings is not going to get you nowhere. Bro, you got to get your story out there. What you got to say is what the streets been missing. Forget about the fantasy in f—— ing Ms. Shoemaker. Utilize that same source of energy in getting one of these COs to be your voice on the other side of the fence. Write you a book, my nigga. Seize the moment. Be productive. You got a better opportunity when people see you trying to do something."

ABL just nodded his head he was in total harmony. His cellmate made sense. ABL was so caught up in thinking one way and one way only. He was drowning so much in sorrow he didn't allow anything else to settle within his mind, let alone writing a novel.

"Insidious," ABL uttered, "more dangerous than seems evident." He smiled. "I like that."


The end.

# ABOUT THE AUTHOR

Alphonso Clement is thirty-eight years old. He was raised in Columbus, Ohio, by a lovely woman, his grandmother, Ms. Eloise Watters. Typically as the story goes, he is a child with no mother and no father in his life. A community made up of choices a lot of times other people are in control of. With that in mind, the author's outlook in life was very bleak. He became hostile and a very problematic child.

Currently the author is incarcerated, where he is able to grace his passion for writing. Recently, he has written a novel titled *Insidious*. It's about a young woman who attempts to carry her father's legacy as a drug kingpin, once her mother and father were brutally murdered in the streets of New York City. Within the years of establishing her name and presence, she obtained an appetite to seek vengeance in the killing of her parents. Despite her cartel connections and billion-dollar network, hate and murder began to boil through her veins. Violence and power became more ideal for this walking beauty, with such a graceful touch, though with bloody hands.